Staff of Laurel, Staff of Ash

Sacred Landscapes in Ancient Nature Myth

Staff of Laurel, Staff of Ash

Sacred Landscapes in Ancient Nature Myth

Dianna Rhyan

MOON BOOKS

Winchester, UK
Washington, USA

JOHN HUNT PUBLISHING

First published by Moon Books, 2023
Moon Books is an imprint of John Hunt Publishing Ltd., No. 3 East Street, Alresford
Hampshire SO24 9EE, UK
office@jhpbooks.net
www.johnhuntpublishing.com
www.moon-books.net

For distributor details and how to order please visit the 'Ordering' section on our website.

Text copyright: Dianna Rhyan 2022

ISBN: 978 1 80341 196 5
978 1 80341 197 2 (ebook)
Library of Congress Control Number: 2022904246

A CIP catalogue record for this book is available from the British Library.

Design: Matthew Greenfield

UK: Printed and bound by CPI Group (UK) Ltd, Croydon, CR0 4YY
Printed in North America by CPI GPS partners

.

We operate a distinctive and ethical publishing philosophy in all areas of our business, from our global network of authors to production and worldwide distribution.

Contents

For Mark
sine quo non

To Nicholas
iam futurus

The hidden harmony is stronger than the obvious one.
(a fragment of Heraclitus)

*These things would come, even if I hid them or
covered them in silence.*
(the prophet Tiresias to Oedipus)

Prologue

Assembled, these pages refused to assemble, and so altogether, they form a series of sketches, fallen like samaras, whose order is ultimately undetermined. The priestess of Apollo wrote her prophecies on leaves. When strong winds came, they scattered all over her cave. Did she mind? Amidst the leaves, voices of winds and voices of trees, lost and found, thread their way. Their tapestry of songs, weaving authentic life, is fading.

> *There remains only a vanishing story, unspoken, of long ago.*
> (Oedipus the King)

Here is a vanished garden not yet illumined by excavation, a scribal tablet house with tumbled shelves, and a goddess' inscrutable archaic smile. The flowering maiden might be taken below—but returns above to live in branching story. Silence might be drawing breath to speak. May these pages speak perilous bright adventure: part memoir of fertile forest floor, part mythic library found in fragments.

Furnace Run

Written in wind and running water.
(Catullus)

Between ancient white oaks who shade an abandoned carriage road nestles a solitary chiseled doorstep. Slantwise beneath the moss, any door it knelt in front of is long gone. I sit beside it above a ravine that the creek called Furnace Run has cut steep, west of the Cuyahoga River. I feel its rough coolness on my hip; it feels my warmth on its flank. We are regarding a remote corner of the Appalachian Plateau.

The stream trickles slender arpeggios; the oaks whisper together in muted tongues.

A dark limb arches overhead, muscled as a dancer's leap. As I listen, twigs crackle their peculiar dialect to neurons and galaxies. Roots curve around my feet, tracing rivulets in the soil, as gravity leads them gently to the deep. Poised against the deepening dusk, oak crowns faithfully sign what their roots have come to know. But not everything; roots hold back some secrets even from their branches above.

Ancient myths hold back secrets from storytellers. What they reserve in silence will never be named. For every archaic story, the words are doubtful. Gaps, ellipses, erasures, mold, fire, a hesitating scribal hand, make every translation tentative.

As I write, lichen samples the doorstep's sandstone. Down the slope lies a ruined cabin, where logged pines and living pines weep resin, kneeling together. Attending them, ivy pulls her green cloak close and ventures an embrace. Dust motes fall, fern roots wind apart, grapevines crumble bricks, and shrub rose tests new legs in garbage pits. In the town nearby, creek beds and backyards bud with millstones heaved from local quarries. Their masons have fled, along with the smelters who once knew

2

this creek. And long before those workmen, people who knew this creek more deeply by far had already been made to vanish. A scant few mortal handiworks, millstones, arrowheads, and doorsteps stay.

The white oak I lean against has stayed, shouldering human steps as we walk across these roots like so many searching ants. Hearing our voices. To the oak, our words are like characters, like the speaking masks of Greek tragedy, or allegories in an antique pageant, hollow for speaking through.

Like all beings who are alive—oak, lichen, shrub rose, and creek—we are cast onto a place, swirled into ephemeral shape, and carried forward to unfathomable purpose. So are our stories. If our place is imperiled, so are our myths. Sacred landscape can be a bank of the Euphrates, a cave in Attica, or the moss beneath my feet. If we heal the one, we heal the other. So said priestesses who long ago spoke in the voice of doves. So said the prophetic oaks they tended, who murmured to their suppliants through windblown leaves.

Here beyond the lichen doorstep, oak leaves lie scattered and fallen in patterns beyond our ken. Crackled brown fragments of distant seasons slumber. On the branch, cloaking the ground, or in a worm's belly, they wait inside their forms.

As protean myths unravel enigmas robed in roots and leaves, may these tattered story scraps inspire us to care for fragmented, neglected places. If we will view a beloved, imperiled place through the eyes of an ancient, fading story, we will see both place and myth together more profoundly.

Sitting in silence, the ear of the heart attends, to hear the stories written in wind and running water.

Samaras

A shrew devours a flailing worm, and maidens dance in disguise for the goddess who guards the shrew's litter. A stone carver visits a remote cave, is captured by its nymphs, and never leaves the place again. The god of wisdom mounts the Tigris River like a bull, and the practice of irrigation is born. A molting doe, soaked with sleet, has vanished into the ravine. Blackberry canes pattern her tracks in a dialect she knows, hieroglyphs we no longer understand.

Each of these images is real—or was once believed to be.

Can myth stop someone from felling ancient oaks? I watch vanished stories unfold afresh as papyrus scrolls, terra cotta figurines, and human bones are excavated from the soil after sleeping for millennia. I wonder at the goddess Artemis, who turned a hunter into a stag for trespassing in a nature preserve. And I contemplate the hero Gilgamesh, axe in hand, who realized what he had done too late for the Cedar Forest.

As a mythologist, I hand over forgotten stories and hope. Those who care for devastated lands heal the underbelly of humankind's relationship with the wild, flowing in real waters and hiding beneath real bones.

To aid them, myth slips in where logic could never go.

How to heal a broken world? Humans have pondered this question at least since the dawn of writing gives us a record to go by. We answered the question too, by telling stories about wolves and moles, shrews and does, blackberries and bulls, goddesses, and gods. And even stories about humans. Questions grow richer when we need not answer them from a single vantage point, alone.

Some questions are seeds; they split. To reach toward life, they fracture. They do this in earth we barely know.

Maple trees grow seeds called samaras that leap free from

stems and whirl in unpredictable loops to the ground. Or into the water. Silver maples I often sit with cast their seeds onto the bank of the Cuyahoga River. There they live or die. The difference between the two paths lies in whether the seed roots fork to go deep, deep as lightning bolts cast down into the danger and wisdom below our feet. There are needful things down there that we have forgotten.

Lanthanein in Ancient Greek means to be forgotten. To escape or elude notice, to be unseen. To disappear while doing something—or seem to. Conversely, it means to forget that something is alive, to forget how to see it, to lose all memory of it. We tell ourselves that we do the forgetting, but forgetfulness is a protection inherent in living things, including sandstone, oak, and story. If we trace roots of words, like roots of plants, we will hear the forgotten notes they resonate below the range of casual hearing. Somewhere beneath our notice, mythic words and sinews stretch, in rocks and streams and trees, to dive and surface and dive again.

As children, we called maple samaras whirlybirds, stretched down to rustle them between our hands, and tossed them high to delight in crazy spirals. Now I know they dash down hollow trails like Homeric princesses on twinkling ankles, like quivering nymphs whose hair swirls with blossoms. In winter I think of them, settled, nosing their way through frost to begin anew the path of maple, or to turn away into the dark.

This is the fertile stark choice—stark enough to germinate myth—that authentic life and beloved places insist on, every season afresh: the choice of turning to be made or remade. Spiraling, rooting, or being swept away. The spiral of healing our inevitable wounds finds its story pattern in the natural world, in whorls of myth and twists of winding trunks.

In conditions of extreme hardship, trees twist, growing wood that winds around the trunk, like a woman whose veil trails over her feet, turning at her waist and shoulders to shelter her face from the wind. The more exposed, the closer the grain spirals, to help the tree be surer on her feet in shedding wind.

Every part of a tree turns from root to crown, searching. Curvaceous heartwood, flesh of the tree, does not lend itself to planks. The harsher the forces they are exposed to, the more oblique they grow. Rather than submit to straightening, boards will warp and split in unforeseen directions. Sent to market, crooked trees are said to have little worth.

Foresters and spirals, trunks and planks, curves, and valuation. I grew up with carpenters who worked in wood. I speak with a local arborist who has risked his job again to defend an oak grove on coveted land. He knows that between every two trees there really is a doorway to a new world. But even if they don't see a doorway, since harvesters find less use for trees with spiral grain, misshapen trees get to twist out of the chainsaw's way. As Thoreau says of a scrubby wild apple tree he admires, though conditions stunt it every season, it does not give in to despair.

Some rivers are called crooked because they have spiraled; they turn and curl and writhe, trying to find safe passage. Such unstraight habits give trees and rivers character.

Kharaktēr in Ancient Greek means an impression that remains. A cipher of chisel that marks stone, an indelible scar from an old wound. A curve that will never be straightened.

Myths have character too. Once we turn toward myth in the wild, the incline may become ingrained. We may be shaped by a bond without apparent goal or value, whose sap flows fainter than whispers, and is never sundered from longing. Enchantment. "Seized by nymphs" is what ancient Greeks called it. As we turn toward maples, they also turn, to track sun, seek water, and find mineral nourishment. They packet what they glean into samaras. They are never still.

In changing all things find repose.
(Heraclitus)

Seeds, roots, branches, and buds are how trees express wisdom now, through seemingly mute silhouette. The oldest oak in a sacred grove was believed silent—until she spoke.

Her story went something like this.

There was a majestic ancient oak who stood in a grove sacred to Ceres, Roman goddess of nourishing grain. Garlands and votive tablets graced her limbs, in her cool shade nymphs danced, and she was mother to the forest all around. But king Erysichthon violated the grove with iron and declared:

Even if this lofty tree is Ceres herself—
not just a tree the goddess loves—
her leafy head will now lie on the earth.
(Ovid's Metamorphoses)

Work began. The oak trembled and groaned out loud. His men stopped working and drew back. But the king did not falter in his blasphemous daring; when one servant tried to stop him, he killed him with his axe. Finally, as he hacked on alone, a voice was heard from the heart of the oak:

I am a nymph of oak, spirit of this tree,
dearly beloved of Ceres.
I prophecy to you with my dying breath:
punishment stands right behind you.
(Metamorphoses)

The tree fell, and in revenge, Ceres cursed the timber-hungry

7

man with deadly and insatiable hunger. His appetite was now relentless as his hatchet once had been. Food he swallowed only awakened his craving for more, yet ravenous eating left him famished, hollow. In the end, in desperation, he consumed himself. That is how Ovid tells it.[1]

When such a nature myth speaks, primal images rise. From oak grove, from twilit library and freshly dug soil, the stories jolt us awake. We meet a king starving to death as he forks from a groaning table. We watch a goddess face down fifty giants. We see a leviathan whose entrails encase a shrine, and witness a water spirit fleeing a fortress, revealed to be woman above and serpent below. Awakened, such beings speak truth in accents capable of shaking us out of our trance, yoked as we may have been to quiet desperation. Committed, even, as we may have been, to our own domestication.

Many tears I have wept for this,
many paths I have wandered deep in thought.
(Oedipus the King)

The ancient voices speaking from these pages viewed the land as a sacred primordial being who was alive with the goddesses and gods of nature. All deities influenced nature. Many dwelt not in temples, but in numinous caves and groves, or roamed free in the form of natural forces like winds, storms, or springs. Because the creative earth was a wise organism, wise humans treated the environment with care and approached the earth with respect. A natural resource had both practical and spiritual meaning. Ancient people did fell trees to build ships and diverted water for irrigation. They plowed, mined, and hunted. An archaic traveler with a speculating eye could look at forest-fringed wildflower meadows and see something quite other than ecosystems.

That island is not a bad place at all.
It is going to waste; only goats go there.
It could yield all kinds of seasonal crops.
The meadows seem well-watered,
Parts of it look rich and ripe, level, and soft for plowing.
Someone there would always harvest deep.
(Odyssey)

Odysseus is speaking, a man richly punished for his mistreatment of Artemis, protectress of pristine land.

Nature's gifts were generous, yet dangerous. A nearby stream was needed as a resource and reverenced as living water. Rivers and mountains could have two names: the divine one, mortals were forbidden to use. Soil was needed for crops yet was also a conduit to the Great Below. Oaths were made powerful by stooping to touch the ground. They could sound like this:

Rivers and Earth, stand as witnesses.
Keep watch over our oaths of fidelity.
(Iliad)

Or even simpler, proverbially, a person could swear:

By earth, by springs, by rivers, by streams.

Ancient wisdom speaks to us today if we keep watch over our fidelity. If we are seeking a sacred antidote or refuge from humanity's ruthless handling of the earth.

Once he had been healed of skepticism, the ancient geographer Pausanias called myth not foolishness, but a strange sort of wisdom. We enter now into strange and silent openings, deer trails branching off known paths, to hear again, to turn toward, the forces of wind, water, soil and sun, the strange and wise enigmas of the wild. To glimpse again the nymphs whose lives

9

are the lives of tree and spring, and trace ridged tree bark and glistening worm trails with feather touch. The word-root *enigma* in Ancient Greek means not only a mystery, but an opaque utterance that requires intuitive wisdom—strange wisdom—to interpret. We are listening for language that provides not an answer but an opening.

Once we have been healed of skepticism, shake off the trance of civilization, and open our ears to hear, voices rise countless as dapples on sycamores or Homeric daughters of Ocean.

Thetis is perceptive, she listens to voices above,
as she sits in the depths of the sea and goddesses gather around her.
Her silvery cave teems with Ocean's daughters,
sea-nymphs, all her sisters. When her son is troubled,
swiftly she surfaces, like mist rising on the face of grey water.
(Iliad)

The swirling multiplicity and compassion of Thetis's cave nourish hope that the ancient sources gathered here—poems, glossaries, dialects, epiphanies, oracles, journals, epitaphs, inscriptions, histories, fragments, and choruses—resonate more fluently than any single tongue ever could. We excavate treasures of darkness: buried stories we meant to go back for, myths almost lost forever, words that say things we no longer can. We must translate the words as a sea nymph would sing them, or as mycelium deciphers stone dust for trees.

Drive Out Nature

As the Sumerian fecundity-of-nature goddess Inanna proceeded to her death through the seven gates of the underworld, surrendering her powers one by one:

> *She asked at each gate,*
> *as each talisman and jewel,*
> *each potency was stripped away,*
> *"Gatekeeper, why is this done?"*

> *Each time the keeper intoned:*

> *"Silence, Inanna.*
> *Do not open your mouth against custom.*
> *The rules of the Great Below are flawless.*
> *You may not question what is perfect."*
> (Inanna's Descent)[2]

The archaic impulse to conquer and domesticate wild fertility rears its head here in the voice of the one who locks massive doors. The underworld is perfect, Inanna is told, and no one may question its rules. But in the myth of *Inanna's Descent to the Netherworld* (named for Ishtar in Akkadian), rules turn out to be strategies to disarm. Perfection can neatly justify mastery and promise a more flourishing life than nature spares. Yet no matter how we name its myriad ways, perfection deadens. In paradise myths, for example, human cravings for ease and immortality are met, and nature is disarmed. As is commonly known from Eve traditions, suspicion of women can flourish in gardens of blissful, infantile yearnings.

As civilization developed, the terrain around settlements, and females within settlements, were identified together as disturbingly wild and in need of control. In ancient Greece, land that was named was considered fatherland, but earth in her natural state was a mother. Girls and women were defined as inherently more connected to the earth. Stories entwine the domination of females and nature as the taming project grew, revealing its two prongs as having one handle. As the Roman poet Horace gendered it:

You can drive out nature with a pitchfork, but she will keep on running back.

This is how water or tree roots behave. Nature powers did not have to be female, as we will see. Rivers, forest guardians, and mountains could also be gods. Whatever their presentation, outsiders needed to be—or be made into—something outside the dominant voice: female, animal, captive, foreigner, nomad, monster, cross-dressing cult performer. Alien others were convenient vessels for projection, to contain odious aspects of the self: dirty, wily, potent, wayward, perilously fertile, and unpredictable. For fear of religious pollution, an ancient sanctuary of Kronos posted a notice:

No women, no dogs, no flies.

Females were, in imaginative terms, storage jars whose lids gapped open, doors that would not stay shut, tablets that said unpredictable things, overly fertile monster-spawners, busybody monkeys or cunning weasels. Unless, that is, they were perfect beings of unquenchable mystery and fertile potential who fed desire: picturesque nymphs always just out of reach, home-loving honeybees, or frisky fillies glancing at bridles and resolute riders. All those images come from ancient poems. As for nature, it—she—could be dirty, monstrous, and unpredictable too: the well that ran dry, the windstorm that flattened the orchard. Unless, that is, nature could somehow pour forth inexhaustible perfection. Surely one of the gifts of myth is to make opposites meet. As Sumerian beer and Roman wine comforted daily pains of unremitting labor, so the legend of a perfect place was intoxicating: an enclosed garden who perpetually yielded her fruits for the asking, where men could be at ease and simply pluck what they wanted.

But what could be more contrary to the reality of cyclical nature? To borrow metaphors from the sage Utnapishtim when he challenged Gilgamesh's futile immortality quest:

Is human strength any more than a reed to be flattened by the wind?
Could a mortal made of clay build anything that would never collapse?
(Epic of Gilgamesh)

That quest was destructive to every form of life Gilgamesh met. Finessed in heroic language, utopian stories of the past carried disturbing undertones. A royal portrait from the palace of Ashurbanipal displays the king and queen picnicking in a pleasure garden. As they toast each other over an artfully arranged table of delectable morsels, an enemy's severed head hangs from the manicured branches of a nearby tree.

While civilization feasted on such hierarchies and hopes, the conquered, enslaved, or domesticated were less likely to picnic on delicacies than to be plucked themselves. Hesiod made it a fable. As the hawk said to the nightingale:

Silence, lady, you puzzle me.
Why do you bother to speak?
Do not make that pitiful noise.
I will make a meal of you if I want to,
or from my curving talons let you go.

Only a fool opposes someone more powerful than she is.
(Works and Days)

For the heavenly and perfect, can we look to the god of justice Zeus, head of his immortal entourage? The thunderbolt of Zeus was called the only unstoppable force in nature. It wasn't. Nature has her own. When his henchman threatened to torture an insubordinate, he claimed that Zeus did not even know the word "alas." But that was never true. Zeus's career in Greece began as lesser consort to a native goddess, and his first entrance in the *Iliad* flashes back to a brush with utter defeat. He was barely saved by silver-ankled Thetis—and the hundred-handed giant by her side. Though Zeus would banish it forever from Olympus, the word "alas" has meaning for all who live.

Justice began as a goddess who deplored corruption:

She weeps when she is dragged around by bribe-devouring hands.
(Works and Days)

Even for Demeter, goddess of plentiful harvest, the illumination of her rituals faced the deep sacrificial pit. Her mysteries for men and women began with daylight processions. But her rites of animal sacrifice were for women exclusively and held only by night. Her ceremonial year journeyed from light to dark and back again, never one without the other.

At her generous touch:

Seed germinates and bursts open in furrows,
land blooms into bountiful vegetation.
(Homeric Hymn to Demeter)

Myth bursts open too. Any goddess's wrath once invoked could be implacable, and then the captivating meets the grotesque.

Inanna makes heaven and earth quiver.
She spits fire, flood, and overwhelming terror.
She spews venom like a dragon, roars like thunder.
She opens the path of lamentation,
and terror leans heavy upon the land.
As she gallops by, standing up on the back of a beast,
no god has any plan to stop her.
(Hymns to Inanna)

In Sumerian proverbs, the city must face the wilderness; it undergirds even the palace. Humanity must face the wilderness; it undergirds houses of clay.

Recovery from appetite for paradise-grown fruit requires turning away from gatekeepers who take and take in attempts to imprison nature's vitality, to find our way back to wild domains, where the strongest bolts spring open. Away from empty-eyed images of perfection, in the muddy crevices of the natural world, something flickers just outside the field of vision, something we can almost hear. Expressed in flawed and frightening myths, enchantment still lives and wanders out there, in every forest remaining on the earth.

Crooked River

Loss and longing resound in echoes of long-ago song.

The Muse inspired the singer to open his exquisite voice,
and they sat spellbound listening in hushed and shadowy halls.
His song was like a god's,
his lyre rang like a bow,
plucked before the shedding of arrows.
His voice rang pure as the voice of a swallow.
(Odyssey)

Homeric singer, lyre, bow, and swallow ring clear, each note a wild, archaic tone.

Arkhē in Ancient Greek means origin and guiding principle, the word-root of archaic and archaeology. This is the opening note of a song that has died away, or the invisible acorn that birthed the visible oak. The archetypal snake swallowing its tail is an image of arkhē, concealing purposes and genesis. If the snake's beginnings are glimpsed, it sloughs off skin to escape definition.

Along the serpentine Cuyahoga River, a river that has notoriously and repeatedly caught fire, whose name seems to mean "crooked," nothing is perfect. The true origin of the word Cuyahoga has been lost through the genocidal displacement and killing of indigenous peoples by Euro-American settler-colonitsts. In what was called the frontier of Ohio, after the near extinction of indigenous speakers and their languages, historical silence grapples with folk memory. Suggestions include a source in Wyandot, Seneca, Cayuga, Erie, or Mohawk expressions. Are any of those true?

Loss and longing sing in this throaty flint-grey river forging muddy oxbows.

When the river beside me burned, paradox reigned, the snake kept its own counsel, and gatekeepers hid the origin of pollution, pursued by their own hounds. No familiar definitions of water made sense, water and fire being opposites of old. Yet already in the archaic epics this unlikely pass had come, in legends of Proteus, old man of the sea, who could manifest as wave or fire at will. And in the poetry of warfare: when a divine river burned by the power of the god of industry, forge, and flame. As the *Iliad* wound to a close, Troy's river god was punished for refusing to swallow human corpses, arrogance, brutality, and pollution. Surely the Cuyahoga River was not punished for refusing to feast. Yet where mortals once poured honeyed wine upon the waters, they turned to pour slag and excrement.

When Heraclitus said, "a beast is driven to pasture by a blow," he meant us.

How can water burn? Kabbalah wisdom foretold that a day would come when language would rise against humankind. On that day, words would cast off the yoke of meaning in our mouths and become their true selves, deaf to definitions.[3]

When that day comes, water could kindle, and the words for water and fire would be free to intermingle. How pitiful that we now believe a river god entrusts his future to us. We, who are molded clay from a riverbank; we who first learned culture from Sumerian fish-sages who emerged from watery depths; we who can barely speak without paradox and forget the name Cuyahoga. We want to remember how to sing songs that do not shed arrows. Even if only in lamentation for the river.

Look back to the Homeric singer whose voice rang clear as a swallow's song, whose lyre resounded like a bow. A play on words is sounding here because the word *bow* (for arrows) sounded like the word for life.

Life gives name to the bow; but the bow come to life is death.
(Heraclitus)

Behind the wordplay stand paradoxical objects we cherish: a lifegiving instrument of song, and a death-dealing instrument of war and the hunt. Like the staff of laurel and staff of ash, we touch one to heal and the other to destroy, and they are linked by our hands in purposeful making.

They come to our hand in turn: the iron weapon and sweet singing lyre.
(Alcman)

What an unlikely pass we have come to: to drink whole lakes, plow down to bedrock, and hold tight to ecosystems to try to make them stop changing and foiling all our plans.

He clung to the sea goddess when she transformed into a bird,
he grasped her by the waist when she became a massive tree,
but suddenly she writhed as a muscular mottled tigress.
Terrified, he released his grip, then tried another tactic.
He poured an offering of wine into the waves.
(Metamorphoses)

That was how a mortal tried to marry Thetis, as Ovid pictured it anyway. How to relax our own grip on the body of tree, tigress, river, word, snake? By what right do we pour into the waters? Ancient medicine imagined women's bodies as sopping places, crisscrossed by rivers that all ran to her womb. Do we somehow imagine that all rivers should run to us to be consumed?

The Hippocratic writer of *Airs, Waters, Places* saw that human health reflected environmental health. Thousands of years afterward, such awareness is often considered something new, while the headlong ruin of ecosystem collapse grows heads

Hydra-like from attempted domination of wild forces, a project that mortals have never grown tired of. How did humankind come to care so little for the earth?

Our power is built on riverbed sand and gravel. Fish-sages, swallows, and rivers might think such tottering thrones unwise. So might poplars and pines.

The tragic king Pentheus, whose name did mean "man of pain," teetered on top a pine tree once, until women enraged by his spying, desperate for freedom from his regime, and driven wild by ritual ecstasy on the mountainside, tore him down. Such steep and sudden downfall in Greek tragedy was called a *katastrophê*—as in the phrase environmental catastrophe.

The name of the goddess Persephone means destroyed voice and voice that destroys.

But she is also called a tender shoot and delicate bud. And anyone who has heard her seasonal myth of spring knows that she is not destroyed. Forgotten or destroyed ones, goddesses, or rivers, do not always stay silent. On riverbanks and meadows, we hearken to the submerged green voice, the stunted seedling, the names of the lost. Water sings, especially in turning, especially in composing lyrics while heaving mossy boulders out of the way. As for Inanna, Persephone, oak tree, or river, the rage of devastation roars inside. While we are looking the other way, the unseen one steals in.

Abyss

Beneath all visible rivers gushes a primordial generative abyss, coursing under the fragile crust we walk on. This dynamic region, or this subsided gargantuan creature, floats between the underworld and the surface shapes we see. One approach to the Great Below is through these waters, which are both boundary and passageway. Places we call unfathomable curve the merest rim on the cup of those fathoms. We all sense that it is there.

The origin of heaven and earth was in those freshwater deeps, when they sprang into being as the children of Nammu, the primordial Sumerian goddess of subterranean waters, who possessed her own fertilizing power for procreation. On the oldest stones and crumbling clay tablets, before the written word, the symbol for sea is Nammu: first one, mother of every god.

The whole universe surged upward out of the Apsu, from the profundity of Nammu's womb. Sumerians called these depths, her depths, the Apsu, progenitor to our word abyss. Apsu was once a living deity, moving unseen in the cavernous freshwater deeps. In later Babylonian tradition, now conceived as male, he flowed as sweet water to female Tiamat's salt; their mingling to create more gods opens creation. But the crafty god Enki poured a spell over the colossal creature until Apsu was drenched with sleep, killed him, then set up his dwelling in the body. Once Enki had vanquished the leviathan, he kept the being's name for both the region of underground waters and his new home there, his twisting and turning, labyrinthine, underwater shrine. From then on, both were known as Apsu.

A shrine Enki founded to be his own,
its vault a roiling inundation,
its passages entrails that echo.
An ulterior shrine he founded,

with halls that twist
like threads not to be followed,
knotted innards
no one except Enki comprehends.
(Enki's Journey to Nibru; Enki and the World Order)

Inside this murky foundation, this renovated womb, Enki listened to hymns. As the newly installed lord of the deep he feasted, designed his living space, lived in splendor, and mated with his lover—all inside an eternally slumbering architectural body. The halls of his shrine still contrived to twist like intestines or rope, conjured from the spell poured out to quench consciousness and still the mighty waters. Enki's innermost sanctum, deep inside Apsu, became his headquarters for designs, decisions, and destinies. Other gods dared not approach it. If the story makes us uneasy as we look out over rolling bodies of water, that is because it is meant to.

To evoke this strange and watery past, Mesopotamian temples dug freshwater pools to pull the Apsu into the present. Archaeologists have excavated a sacrificial layer of fish bones from the subterranean levels of his oldest shrine at Eridu. When Enki rises, fish rise around him in waves.

If we return to the antediluvian fish-men, those culture heroes emerged from and disappeared back into the teeming depths of the sea. They made their dripping epiphany before worldwide inundation, before the divinely sent Flood. They imply that our cultural forms are like mighty Apsu: prone in troubled slumber or deathlike submission, awaiting a day to come when they will shake off servitude. The first sage was a son of Enki who held the god's priesthood above the fishbone floor in Eridu. He rose out of the sea in hauntingly evolutionary form.

Were you there that day? One head fish, the other man.
Walking on human feet, fishtail on the sand behind.

We did not understand his language—how did he know ours?
We were wandering naked, hungry, artless, and didn't mind,
A handful of wild barley, a drink from a pond, and
didn't know any better. He came in close to teach us
face to face. But did anyone ever see him eat or sleep?

"Here is how to gather fruit,
here is how to prepare it—no, I am not hungry.
Here is how to build a house,
and dwell inside—no, I will not sleep."

Though he did not do the things that make for kinship,
every day that year, when the sun rose, he rose from the waves.
With every sunset, the wise amphibian sank into the deep.
We forgot we had ever learned anything on our own.
Maybe we hadn't. A year and a day went by,
and one morning he did not reappear, though we waited.
Sometimes he flashes quicksilver through a memory,
But we stopped searching the shore, and never saw him again.
(Berossus' History of Babylonia; The Debate Between Sheep
and Grain) [4]

Born of Nammu, we human beasts, once sea dwelling, once amphibious, draw breath on land still mesmerized inside frameworks the fish-sage supplied. We learned arts and crafts and swam in new knowledge. Are letters, laws, and words in servitude to us, or do they help entrance us in mazes of cunning device, unable to follow Oannes into the depths of reality? Although he taught defining, measuring, and knowing, in his own body he was quicksilver, mysterious, and apart. He refused the intimacy of breaking bread or sharing a roof with us, and he required regenerative nocturnal depths to saturate his daytime labors. We come away from the advent of this creature with the sense that something in his watery source understands the human voice, and could choose to use it in careful measure, while we understand only a fading version of his titrated wisdom.

The Apsu was named for Apsu. How curious. A souvenir? I look out over a slope where oaks have been excised; the place is called Oak Hill. I visit a place called Hidden Springs; all the springs have dried away.

Moving between realms with curious double locomotion, the aquatic sage is both us and not us. Among other revelations, he heralds the transition between gratitude for whatever the earth bestows, and purposeful planting and harvesting. This son of Enki, sent to appraise but not to join us, is amphibious and ambiguous from all sides. Perhaps he had to be. Among his many inventions, Oannes's father Enki devised the first fishhook, whose gleaming curve charms fish to swallow its point and be hauled up gasping out of the Apsu.

Out of the water, following the fish-sage, there still swim predatory stories of how human consciousness evolved. According to one modern song of remembering, the need to hunt first led oceanic cells to entwine. Then once up on the watery marsh, resource-stalking led animals, fungus and plants down paths that profoundly diverged.

This entangled tale floats like a jellyfish, crawls like a walking catfish, and entices our imagination from the marshes to the waves, back down into the Apsu. Something there is meditating on ourselves as predatory sea creatures, surrounded by beings who swam up beside us out of Nammu, devising clever implements and furrows that curve back upon our own bellies. I think of a recently discovered Hemimastix branch of protists on the tree of life, watery predators who swim awkwardly by design, because their limbs have evolved to function as pointed harpoons. Have they forgotten that they once knew how to swim weaponless among the other children of Nammu? Have we?

Fish and human embryos both have gill arches and begin life looking like worms. We swim in an aqueous environment to gestate within the womb of our mother, and share more than we suppose with catfish, worms, fungus, amphibians, germs... and samaras too.

Before joining the Cuyahoga River, Chippewa Creek washes knees of cedars and undercuts banks of abandoned farms, then cascades newly freed from a Victorian dam. Nearby, the library is hushed and sunlit like avenues of tree shelves, books nestled in shadowy branches. Questions about water can be sought there in biology or hydrology. Antique maps hibernate in the archive room. But sacred landscape is down by the water, in the mysterious element for the advent and disappearance of wisdom. Hidden behind a sandbar, leaves tumbled under and churned by rock resurface to float long dreaming across a quiet side pool, the layered grey shale filtering reflected light off slick roots of gnarled sycamores. Then they disappear, swept on. A few fishermen wade in with poles.

If we are to glimpse Oannes in this valley, it will be on the bank of a flooded creek like this one.

Withdrawal, Devastation, Return

From banks of collapsing clay, an outlier sets off to follow the stream to its source. Willing or unwilling, aware, or unaware, this is the way to the collective depths beyond and beneath the Apsu. There lies the Great Below. There end all paths.

A newborn boy.
When he was not quite three days old,
the king had servants pierce and tie his ankles together,
and throw him out on a remote and trackless mountain.
(Oedipus the King)

Behind this suppressed remembrance of Oedipus's infancy lies not only an individual memory, but the parental practice of infant exposure, known from myth and history. As I write, excavation is ongoing in the ancient Agora Bone Well in Athens, and on other sites where very young humans and animals were thrown, perhaps living, perhaps dead. Out-cast was a literal word.

The living one who enters into quest may be a social outcast, or may be a hero who ventures forth to fortify his reputation. Or a celestial goddess may decide to direct her steps into the wild, curious about underground ideas she has been advised to ignore. The decision to set out is not only a matter of self-determination; fate plays a powerful hand. In the netherworld, the Anunna gods survived, dread judges and primordial pronouncers of fate. Demons swarmed here. Some had no ears to hear petitions for forgiveness or hands to receive offerings, sincere or insincere. Like cicadas who spend all but a brief span underground and never feed above, they had no mouths. These mythic beings drank no outpourings of atonement. Perhaps they even had hooklike cicada legs, since they clung fiercely to any would try to leave and could not be brushed away. In

25

other words, this path does not swerve or double back. Abyssal depths offer assurances to no one.

In the beginning, near the advent of Oannes, when ovens had just learned to bake bread, Enki attempted to use the Apsu as a conduit: to dive down through the abyss to enter the underworld realm of the goddess Ereshkigal. But Apsu's water is protective. As he plummeted, he was opposed by creaturelike storms.

When Enki set sail for the underworld, tempests fought him off.
Sledgehammers pounded the king; they struck in the form of hail.
Siege engines lashed the intruder; they advanced in the form of sleet.
Reptiles charged, wolves closed in tight, lions leapt at his face.
They moved in the shape of waves, they stormed in swells, that tried to swamp his boat.
(Gilgamesh, Enkidu, and the Netherworld)

Opaque and unknowable, the region rejects any attempt to spy out its secrets or make it a shortcut to encounter the goddess of death. Since "boat" was a Mesopotamian metaphor for genitals, reaching the shore could mean sexual union. We might pause and reflect anew when stepping out onto the planks of a bridge, cresting the waves in a boat, or plunging into a lake. In this myth, penetration is rebuffed.

Enki's attempted descent reveals the first stage of what would become the archetypal mythic journey. In the sequence of Withdrawal, Devastation, and Return, one of the world's oldest and most profound surviving mythic patterns, a traveler is drawn away from community, pursues a quest to a mysterious land, suffers and faces tests, experiences a symbolic death, and ultimately returns.

Wherever sounded—ringing through a Mesopotamian temple, shared in a modern therapist's office, or sung around a Bronze Age hearth—withdrawal, devastation, and return correspond to manifest triple rhythms in nature, the designer of all patterns. Summer, winter, and spring; birth, death, and increase; waxing, waning, and dark of the moon; maiden, mother, and crone. A triple-faced goddess guards the place where three roads meet.

The descent of Enki in his underwater boat shows him starting out, but we don't know if the embattled god made it to the underworld or not. As we have seen, Inanna did journey all the way there. When she meets her sister Ereshkigal, the death goddess who rules the realm, Inanna, the bold goddess of sexual urges, ecstatic pleasure, and bone-crushing war, is killed. Yet Inanna faced her underground sister, her shadow self, and returned to the upperworld alive.

She sought the path never taken.
She challenged the seven gates.

The underworld queen's allies responded.

Ranks of infernal diseases leapt against the intruder.
The Anunna transfixed her with a level stare.
They shouted against her a hateful verdict,
a fatal word.
(Ishtar's Descent to the Netherworld; Inanna's Descent)

Inanna collapsed and was fastened to a peg on the wall as punishment and trophy. The dazzling goddess of fertility looked like a deflated bag hanging limp; the ravishing goddess of mating looked like a rotted haunch of meat.

"Nothing to fear in death," Epicurus counseled wisely. This is true in a philosophical sense, but a haunch of meat might forget this in the face of Ereshkigal. Inanna confronts a goddess whose hair shivers and twists like snakes or rotten leeks, who writhes on the floor in shrieking abandonment, who plots to

27

condemn, deceive, trip up, and entrap. She was enraged at all who approached.

Does Ereshkigal remember the day they allotted bright heaven and grain-giving earth between themselves and gave her the underworld to be happy with her dowry? Luminous, she had to learn how to breathe roots and worms without choking. How to look steadily in her shadowed mirror and find the snakes in her hair. After a while her lungs could strain solid darkness. Husbands, even immortal ones, died or escaped. After some time, humans pouring lustrations aboveground helped. The seeping marks of deeply filtered draughts stretched into stains she used to find her way. After a while she could see in darkness visible. She listened to the snakes, understood, and let them come and go. "The path that leads up and the path that leads down are one and the same," Heraclitus said. She knew that. But she made sure no goddess or hero ever left unscathed.

It turns out Inanna is her sister's match. Fertility is not squeamish.

> *Inanna, your merest thought hones keen outcomes.*
> *Wild cow, you bear down to depose the haughty:*
> *single-handed, you halter a mountain.*
> *Utter one syllable, and a thriving city is emptied of its people,*
> *snakes and jackals alertly patrol the streets.*
> *Busy canals grow sluggish with sediment,*
> *long grass entangles deserted doorsteps.*
> *The land you turn your face from, fails.*
> (Hymns to Inanna; The Cursing of Agade)

Through strategic planning with shrewd and outcast allies, and wordplay of her own, Inanna did return to live again. But not the same. Who could rise unchanged?

When she turned to leave the throne room,
the Anunna barred the door.
"Whoever enters the dark house stays —
she has seen too much.
You must leave something here as sacrifice,
something that leaves a scar.
No one ascends unscathed."
(Inanna's Descent)

Only the one who suffers, learns. Only the one who learns, survives: a pair of axioms from Greek tragedy. The narrative pattern of withdrawal, devastation, and return is prehistoric. The threefold pattern explores transitions crucial to survival — survival of events deadly enough that sacrifice and scarring are inevitable, and any future seems impossible. We stand today facing environmental apocalypse, seeking a path of healing. Laments in ruins call for restoration of the tumbled places.

Descent we know. Withdrawal and devastation we have witnessed.

The land you turn your face from, fails.

Invisible roots and dead languages remember the realm of trembling below and recall our mode for return. If we rise again, we will have faced the shadow self within ourselves, and the fragility of our lives, brief as an insect's afternoon.

I watched a skittish damselfly alight on a floating twig
and perch iridescent, drifting on the river's face,
eyes contemplating the sun. It twitched,
all aquiver, abdomen angled for flight.
Suddenly, a ripple.
It was gone.
(Epic of Gilgamesh)

Ancient legends spin flaxen threads that lead us, hand over hand, through winding places. Can they lead us through this labyrinth too? If we take a story line in our palms, we find the cord is a long-lived relative of root and knows how to make passage through darkening depths of time.

A single word in Ancient Greek encompasses withdrawal, devastation, and return:

Katabasis, a path of descent, a journey to the underworld, the descent of an idea into the mind.

All seeds retain memory of the journey below.

Expedition to the Cedar Forest

A weapon's own will can draw a man forward.
(Odyssey)

The Mesopotamian hero Gilgamesh had an idea that descended into his mind. Or even an obsession: a quest to Cedar Mountain, to conquer its gruesome guardian Humbaba, and turn the monster's cherished trees to timber. Gilgamesh was hopeful; if Humbaba turned out to be truly lethal, maybe he could call the expedition a *katabasis*.

The Standard Version of the *Epic of Gilgamesh* is Babylonian. But older, fragmentary exploits of the hero languish in obscurity, little read.[5] The fragments, parts of larger mythic cycles about Gilgamesh, are more poignant today than when they were composed. All the overlapping sources describe Humbaba's attempts to protect the sacred forest and his failure in the face of the axe-wielding king. The earlier variants feature a crueler Gilgamesh and tell a more graphic story of deforestation. It is the story of *katastrophê* in a sacred landscape.

Just as mystery surrounds the historical or mythical semi-divine king of Uruk called Gilgamesh, the Cedar Forest is a mystical place, partaking of both real and mythic elements. When the expedition draws near it, briars reach out to detain them and thorns impede their feet. As early kings created parks called "paradises" to protect landscapes and trees for private use, early temples maintained pristine forests, and declared them forbidden to profane steps: sacrosanct down to every rock and tree. Emperors protected woodland where stone boundary markers threatened trespassers, including any who trespassed against cedars. All this means that rich groves featured in ancient religious and imperial decrees. Legislation meets myth at the dawn of conservation.

31

But one by one, trees fell. Elites craved palaces; fleets coveted ships. And every household had a fire for its hearth. Deforestation that began in the Neolithic age was noticeable in antiquity. Persistent imagery of the Garden of Eden shows a forest, with cleared land threatening to encroach from outside the precinct. Plato already saw denuded land in Greece and described it:

Topsoil is eroding and disappearing down into deep sea. Compared with the land before, what is left looks like the skeleton of a sick man, all bones, with the rich and soft earth washed away; only ribs and ridges remain.
(Critias)

This sounds familiar. After millennia of logging, the cedars of Lebanon are remnants struggling to survive. Their fate, decreed or un-decreed, is unknown.

The cedar guardian Humbaba was an imposing ogre of menacing size, impressive teeth, brute strength, and potent auras. His baleful face resembled tangled worms or coiled intestines. Maybe after glimpsing him at a distance, no one bothered to find out how dangerous he really was. Maybe his patron Enlil, father of gods and destinies, knew that Humbaba was as monstrously ugly as he was gentle with his trees, but thought all comers would seek permission and be turned back before they ever dared to encounter him.

He hears a furtive footstep from a mountain range away.
The trespasser's heart flinches and wallows in fear.
The gnash of his bloody jaw brings on paralysis.
One look at his face numbs — it brings on rigor mortis!
Who could face him? You?
(Gilgamesh Epic)

We know from archaeological excavations that Mesopotamians wore amulets of Humbaba's grimace to ward off evil, apparently hoping that even demons would flee his grotesque face. In legend, his mere presence stunned an adversary into passing out helplessly on the ground. Surely the whispering cedars, so peaceful, lofty, and remote, would be safe with vile Humbaba, father Enlil, and sanctified ground to shield them.

Besides, Humbaba possessed seven deadly auras, radiant protective powers.

In Babylonian creation myth, Tiamat gives birth to monsters and bestows radiant auras upon them. This awe-inspiring vital power is *melam*, a force that accompanies Humbaba like a retinue, or even emanates from him: a sheen, resonance, or radiance inherent in deities, temples, demons, or kings. *Melam* caused the beholder to shiver when it vibrated inside exciting artifacts or enveloped intense forms of life. Apsu was imbued with it; Marduk wore it on his brow; Enki killed to possess it. It resided within Inanna's loincloth. Beauty, youth, joy, prowess, and sexual vigor all emit this dazzling wonder.

Melam is the animation of the natural world, barely contained inside artifacts. It is also the vibration of sentient materials, retaining life force, crafted into objects to call upon or amplify that force. Musical instruments resound on their own in Enki's mystical shrine. "A weapon's own will can draw a man forward" is a proverb for arrows eager to bite their target, for swords that should be hidden away.

Such powers were especially vigorous when concentrated in a sacred grove. Temple sanctuaries and their mantles of forestland inspired awe. Holy refuges, they sheltered mystery, and harbored forces of life. Precincts forbade casual entry, and pollution was originally a religious term to describe the aftermath of transgression. In the Cedar Forest, the ogre's auras might have looked like shimmering cloaks or luminous rays around his body. But from Humbaba's perspective, they looked like the limbs of cedar trees.

To my mind, these auras embody forces we still wonder at: inscrutable fates alive on the flanks of shining mountains and in the recesses of submerged caverns. Influences that cause some mountaineers to fall and underwater divers never to return, while others reach home perfectly safe. I have led groups of hikers conversing on the trail who spontaneously grow silent when they enter a deep hemlock grove and remain mute for the rest of the trek. What silences them? To the ancient imagination, a wild frontier like the Cedar Mountain possessed the power to ward off sacrilege and repel invaders, and that power was alive.

But it could be killed.

No one had faced Humbaba like this. When Gilgamesh arrives with his axe, the monster's *melam* stuns the expedition party from afar and leaves them comatose on the ground. Yet Humbaba does not harm them while they lie helpless. His auras seem to work on their own accord, to stupefy the invaders and terrify them to retreat.

When Gilgamesh wakes up, he realizes that he will not elude a sentry equipped with *melam*, so he decides to defeat Humbaba by playing on his affections. He will employ cunning to deprive the giant of his auras one by one. He calls upon Enki's wordcraft, and deception works—because the dread Humbaba reveals himself to be naïve and lonely.

Who bore me? Who raised me?
Echoing mountain caves.
(Gilgamesh and Humbaba)

In a pitiful series of tricks, the monster surrenders each of his radiant powers in return for a sense of belonging. Gilgamesh places both hands on the ground and swears a great oath by the life of his mother and father. He swears the time-honored oaths of earth, sky, and mountain. He has no plan to honor them. One aura is stripped from the orphan with a promise of kinship; Gilgamesh offers Humbaba his little sister as a concubine. Another is destroyed by an oath of lasting loyalty. Other auras are surrendered for promised gifts that represent city sophistication, undreamt of by an isolated rustic: sandals, processed flour, semi-precious stones.

The scene is all too reminiscent of colonial trade of low-value goods for precious natural resources, and promises made to indigenous peoples, never to be kept. It also evokes Inanna as she was stripped of a power at each of the seven gates. As each of Humbaba's auras is traded away, a startling transformation takes place.

The companions who followed Gilgamesh trample into the forest, lop off the aura's branches, tie them up, and stack them at the foot of the mountain.

As the emanations are surrendered, *melam* materializes. Each ray instantly turns into a cedar tree that axmen chop up and truss into bundles. The metamorphosis expresses the bald fact of lumber: bereft of life, cedar trees become cedar wood. Behind this scene stand humans with their first axes, anxious about murdering the *melam* of trees, aware of guilt when they trespassed in eerie groves. Anxious about the forced rite of passage into death when a cedar is felled into a log.

Afterward, denuded of auras as the Cedar Mountain is naked of trees, Humbaba retreats. But Gilgamesh followed him. Pretending to lean close with affection like a brother, instead of a kiss or an embrace, Gilgamesh struck him instead, then tied him up.

Like a bull to slaughter,
like a fledgling stolen from the nest,
like a hostage dragged from home.
(Gilgamesh and Humbaba)

Humbaba sits on the ground and weeps. Not only for himself, but for what he had betrayed—the cedars who provided his only home, and the exuberant life of *melam* they shared.

Before setting out for Cedar Mountain, Gilgamesh persuaded the god of justice to approve his quest. The close of the myth invites us to sit with Humbaba on the ground, to search for justice in what the king of Uruk has done. When the king Naram-Sin plundered a sacred site:

He tore down sacred cedar,
cypress, juniper, and boxwood.
The ground gaped at profanity
against the sanctuary,
against the holy shrine.
In payment for his sacrilege,
the entire city staggered.
(The Cursing of Agade)

Once ancient temples and their nature preserves were set aside as sacrosanct, severe penalties for desecrating sacred land were prescribed by law. Any violence on holy ground was pollution that could be paid for with death. Yet Gilgamesh's plans for the Cedar Forest include not only demolishing the sacred grove and harvesting lumber to build a palace for himself, but also the erection of stone monuments on the site—also to himself. Through tablets of clay and stone:

A name to live forever I will establish there.
(Gilgamesh Epic)

He will set up his own name alongside gods' names on terra incognita, where no titles have yet been established. In Oannes's terms, he will harness words to serve conquest. In modern terms, he will plant his flag to identify, label and claim cleared sites.

Chiseled monuments repeat what their artificer tells them to say. Anticipating the expedition, shouting in the streets, Gilgamesh had already granted himself a new title: "cedar-smiter." He is talking like a god, and the titles of gods were legion. Enki's word was a hair-raising, irrefutable command. Zeus' word was called unerring, and Jupiter's word was *fata*, fate. While Gilgamesh's followers flattered him and helped him plan his monuments, how could Humbaba have learned to read? He stood imbued with the vigor of vibrant life energy, illiterate, un-strategic, bound to the place. As unwilling or unable to run away as a cedar tree was. Indigenous defender of uncharted territory, he challenged Gilgamesh's environmentally destructive and sacrilegious quest. And did not live to sound out the words when the news appeared in stone.

After the hero slaughtered the guardian of the Cedar Forest to harvest protected trees for timber, he reported his triumph to Humbaba's patron Enlil. Gilgamesh tosses Humbaba's head on the ground and stands, expecting praise.

But Enlil is furious. He sees through Gilgamesh.

You should have honored the Cedar Guardian,
you should have greeted him as a friend.
Why have you killed Humbaba?
Did you plan to erase his name from legend,
and substitute your own?
(Gilgamesh and Humbaba)

Enlil knows Gilgamesh cannot answer without incriminating himself. Anyway, the damage was already done. The legendary cedars of Lebanon had begun their slow and incremental decline. Enlil's response to Gilgamesh urges us to look down at our own hands: thousands of years later we are still holding his axe. Or are we in its grip?

Back to the Cedar Mountain, to Humbaba's final moments.

Defeated, Humbaba cried out. Gilgamesh had sworn friendship by heaven, by earth, by mountains, by his own parents, by the name of the underworld.

The ogre reached for his captor's hand, and laid face down in defeat. For a moment, the hero felt pity, and spoke with his henchman and alter ego Enkidu. But they shored each other up, remembering that this is a quest for glory. Humbaba's words have stung; Enkidu feels belittled. Not so long ago, Enkidu himself had roamed the wilderness; he had never tasted ale, bread, or meat; he had never worn a garment. As a recent convert to civilization, he is zealous. He will not hear mercy. In fury, he cuts off the guardian's head.

The beheading scene bracketed by two heroes became a prized tableau for palace art.

But spattered ravines and mountains were his mourners, and wept.
(Epic of Gilgamesh)

In one of the lesser-known fragments, the expedition to Cedar Mountain to wipe out the ranger and his trees began with the words *Ho, Hurrah!*[6] It is the enthusiastic shout of the expedition, the fifty youthful bodyguards. Maybe this is their motto. They had volunteered back in Uruk, when Gilgamesh blew the trumpet to summon men who were expert fighters, unbound by ties to family. Today, their high spirits may sound hollow or chilling: mortals trying not to feel awe in the shadow of a forest they mean to level. Their adrenaline is high—are they shouting to shore up humanity's courage for the devastation to come?

Ho, Hurrah!

The refrain rings out now on our own expedition to deforest the entire earth. Who could oppose that axe?

The Mother of God

The Mother has given arkhē to everything we see.
Chaos alone walked before her in procession.

Behind her iconostasis, the intricately carved altar screen, shaded by marble columns, rests the archetypal mother, her sanctuary settled around her in repose. She is queen of heaven, celestial star of the sea, imperishable fruit tree, and blossom of the rose. In the sacred icon before me now, she enigmatically gestures toward her son. In this pose, she is known as revealer of the path, pointing to a meaning beyond the power of art to convey. Hidden in the countryside down a remote muddy lane, empty of worshippers, even on its own accord the chapel resounds with hymns. In her, opposites harmoniously combine, fertile virgin and mother.

Her archetypal icon is a living image, an ideal that lives in the mind. It is a portal for epiphany, the miraculous manifestation of divinity to a human witness on earth. Epiphany is willingness to unveil in authentic encounter. It can spring from a sacred image, or from an archaic hymn.

She stood there silent, looking down, her eyes veiled.
But then, at a moment of her own choosing,
Demeter transforms her stature,
sheds her disguise and shines forth clothed in beauty.

Delectable fragrance drifts from her aromatic robe,
immortal radiance glows from her luminous face,
lustrous hair cascades around her shoulders.
She flashes brilliant as a bolt of lightning.

Her beholder is struck speechless.
(Homeric Hymn to Demeter)

How to draw near? Her meadow was *abaton*, never to be trodden; her innermost sanctum was *adyton*, never to be entered. When Odysseus described a nymph-haunted cave, he noted two entrances—one forbidden. The cave had twin portals that issued divergent fates.

Inside trickles ever-flowing water. The cave has two mouths.
One in the north wind, where people descend,
the other in south wind, too sacred for mortal feet.
No men enter that way. That is the path of immortals.
(Odyssey)

Where the mother consents to appear, she directs our gaze away from the shallows and toward the depths. In groves that she creates, her branching icon gestures toward the eternal, the door we must all enter.

In her presence, I remember wandering nearby one winter, leaning up on tiptoe to lick an icicle, finding frozen sweetness dripping from twigs of maple. In ancient Egyptian art, tree goddesses pour libations and offer a suckling breast.

By whatever name, between worlds she protects a doorway that opens only from within, as an act of mercy. In a momentary outpouring of mutual delight, outside the chapel, the land resounds.

I sing of shapely Earth, eldest genetrix.
She nurtures everything that lives.
Her grace fills all creatures that creep on land,
all that stir in the deep or soar through the air.
O robust one, you are the cradle of healthy children
and generous bounty of luscious fruit.
You smile on mortals, and they live.
You frown on them, and they die.

Blessed is any life you choose to favor.
(Homeric Hymn to Earth)

Ancient worshippers sang such hymns and prayed her to open her ear, convey a petition, make intercession.

Perhaps she would. Perhaps she would not. Her reasons are inaccessible. A shrine can feel inhabited, or a shrine can feel abandoned. Either way, the divinity's presence or absence is made known. Lightly she moves in and out of the wild. Today, she is here.

Her icon is bathed in muted light from a narrow window with a view to the meadow beyond. She gestures toward her son, and to an oblique window beyond, a narrow slit in the south wall.

She points beyond prayers, to a border of the field just visible beyond the sanctuary window. I follow her gesture. A doe and her fawn have just melted from the frame, into the border, to rest concealed by bare shrub rose and blackberry canes. I glance away, and when I look back, they are silently gone. I am left in the shrine as one who has glimpsed—or thought she had glimpsed—a doe and her fawn molting winter, willing spring.

This last raw edge of frost is when hellebore blossoms appear. Her petal cheek is beautiful, her forage death to deer. Sprung from the tears of the shepherdess Madelon, who wept because in her poverty she had no gift for the holy infant, her leaves are trimmed in frost lined shawls. Her slender neck arches, contemplating her own snow-trimmed ankles.

The neglected meadow's edge is their iconostasis. There is distant music there, played for the Madelon and the fawn.

Let me hear your pure voice, goddess,
sing the holy source of life.
Her music rings faraway in the wild,
echoing faintly into stillness.

The wail of wolves is her melody,
the growl of lions her descant.
Hidden glens and secluded valleys
shelter her delight.
She is the mother of all the gods.
(Homeric Hymn to the Mother of the Gods)

That hymn dies away too, and the empty chapel dwells in wild solitude. All seems textured with quiet, like a worn wise-woman's apron or altar cloths woven by local hands. Outside, a willow fence leans beside a small garden, slanted as stalks of brown winter aster, with spaces to let all creatures in. It must have been wattled mainly to show that even a bedraggled garden is sanctuary.

The holy one might be found betimes in an enclosed garden if it was cultivated with devotion in her honor, but she was never cloistered or biddable. Fortifications of stone were willow woven fences to her, that she entered and left at will. When her image was carried in yearly procession to be bathed in living water, renewed virginity returned with her to her shrine. Purity described her essence, not her history.

Visiting monastic women as a pilgrim, I am struck by the way they view the present moment as timeless, by their equation of today with a day millennia ago. Not that they are remembering Mary's presentation at the temple, for example, but living it ever for the first time with her. Drawn into candlelight and ritual, time becomes irrelevant.

Speak, and the moment passes.

Vows of silence enclosed her rituals and aligned them with the landscape, with individual trees, grottoes, and springs. The wise wove willow fences around naming any of these out loud. In time to come, it is understandable that the pious refused to utter holy names, or betray roots, rocks, and fonts. Refusal was necessary, protective, and absolute. In daily life, sacred silence guarded against drawing any divinity's attention at an unintended moment. Muteness also signified the impossibility of speaking about the sacred in a context that did not comprehend. Spiritual commitment to silence was akin to the silence of the forest, impossible to frame in human speech.

Through the years, sacred wells of saints like St Winifred or St Keyne have embraced silent devotions and held them close for seekers. Tree boughs overhanging holy wells still flutter in the breezes of rural shrines, with strips of fabric tied to female hopes, where a girdle of the holy one might be borrowed from the altar to swell breasts for a hungry infant. Her freshness, integrity, and beauty are one with this place. Devotion here is visible, tangible, and whole.

A doe places nimble hooves around the quivering fawn at her belly. A hemlock poised on tiptoe shelters delicate ferns at her feet.

Nature loves to hide.
(Heraclitus)

In this sanctuary, as the swaying rose and blackberry canes grow still, and the last trailing vine closes to cover deer-prints in the border, I would say, Nature is most herself in concealment. And so is the Mother of God.

The god whose oracle is in Delphi
does not reveal or conceal.
He gives signs.
(Heraclitus)

The goddess whose presence is in this sanctuary neither reveals nor conceals. She gestures.

Naked in the Underworld

"Gatekeeper,
bolt the seven portals to the house of darkness,
then take your time to let each door scrape open.
Go ahead. Permit her entrance.
But make her subject to our sacraments.
Remove every display of her divinity,
each emblem of majesty and ornament of office.
Let the queen of highest heaven enter —
she who thought to threaten me —
crouched before my throne, exposed."

It was done. He bolted each gate behind her.
Naked, crouching low on bended knees,
Inanna crept toward the cavern throne.
(Inanna's Descent)

Inanna naked in the underworld is a stripped and bundled cedar, a cultic tree shorn of votive offerings, a statue toppled and bare of ornament, or a sacred spring mowed of shimmering ferns.

Ritual nudity is powerful. Ancient sculptors knew it. In Mesopotamia, nudity in sacred contexts exposed the beholder to truth without its customary veils of illusion. In processions and temple recesses, vigorous bodies shone, impermanent in flesh and stone and clay.

Bronze Age statues of nude bird-faced goddesses cupping painted breasts seemed repulsive to some modern discoverers. But we know that beauty is in the eye of the beholder. And maybe the statues meant to repulse.

The goddess went below because she was curious, because she recognized that the upper world was not the only world, and because she wanted to bring the insights of darkness to her people. She had already matched wits with Enki to bring foundational boons to her city. Then she submitted to her stark *katabasis* to death. In all her forms, the one who urges seedlings to spring up from the soil is mourned when she disappears. Humbaba sat on the ground and wept for those who had vanished into the Great Below.

Mythic builders dared to probe the naked earth's secrets. Historical builders did too, but with misgivings. We find their tools scattered beside copper foundation pegs cast in the form of snarling lionesses. Their outstretched paws protect curse tablets. When Enki undertook to organize the world and supervise the building of the first temple, he ventured to open the earth with his pickaxe:

The great prince took measurements with his pickaxe,
made a plumb bob of the hoe, and digging began.
The earth was penetrated,
like soft cloth that absorbs a liquid sacrifice.
(Enki and the World Order)

Mortals needed discretion to disturb the ground. Tools for digging offended the earth with probing, and therefore needed awesome power and the promise of a god's protection. The builder who laid structural foundations could attain heroic status for daring to set down mortal works in the earth. He might be sacrificed, then buried and worshipped as a hero, to safeguard the first-laid stones. Masons who dug foundations found themselves not only underground but uncomfortably close to the underworld. Earthy powers repelled them. For all these reasons, Enki deputized a brickmaking and building god. And the implement for primordial construction was a keen-edged tool that plunged as fearsomely as a mythical serpent who was hungry to eat corpses.

Lord of many names and crafts,
brickwork endures beneath your staff and scepter.
You supervise all furrows, bring plow to marry earth,
and fix foundations in place.
(Enki and the World Order)

When Inanna approached the cavern throne of Ereshkigal, she had already, prior to descent, formulated her own rescue plan. Her close companion, divine Ninshubur, was to self-mutilate according to funereal custom: to tear at her clothes, skin, and hair, and smear herself with dust. Scratched, ragged, and filthy, she was to appear weeping before the gods as a mourner, beat a drum, and chant the following lament that Inanna taught her:

O Fathers, do not let anyone
trap Inanna in the underworld.
Do not let anyone stain your precious silver
with grime of the land below.
Do not let anyone take your precious lapis lazuli
and shatter it into pieces of debris.
Do not let anyone saw up your precious boxwood
like lumber scraps thrown on a carpenter's heap.
O Fathers, do not let anyone
slay the young and holy maiden, bright Inanna.
(Inanna's Descent)

Ninshubur was to plead with the gods for Inanna's life as if Inanna were, among other treasures, a boxwood plant: a small, evergreen, living shrub (*Buxus sempervirens*, "ever vigorous"). We know that Inanna's willowy frame was the elegant curve of the date palm trunk; her sweetness was abundant date clusters, sheltered within her orchard and storehouse. When she walked the earth, the perfume of flowering plants was the breath of the goddess.

Ninshubur pleads mercy for what we might suppose

inanimate: tarnished silver, broken stone, sawn-up boxwood. The message to the father-gods is this: do not allow the precious Inanna to be seen as a neglected cult statue made from silver, stone, or wood, as base material, or as an icon that is not alive. Inanna needed honor to survive. As did all the Mesopotamian gods. As do boxwoods, and every other organism that lives.

It is hard to believe that we are in any position with our own fragrant boxwoods other than on our knees before them in lament and supplication. And yet, not so long ago while driving, I saw the phrase "purveyors of standing timber" on a billboard. Standing timber? A modern paradox. It took me driving on for a moment to realize it meant trees. Living trees, the way an animal becomes livestock, a weight of meat, or a goddess is pegged to a wall. The Cedar Forest as so many board-feet and planks; the shrine empty or the god's face turned away.

Long eons have passed between the boxwood, cedar, and us. At some point, we became oblivious; we began to consider trees as things and define them by their uses. Or we started to alternate between seeing them as alive and not alive.

Gilgamesh's lieutenant Enkidu was uneasy about the difference between living trees and wood. In the expedition to Cedar Mountain, he helped fell the noblest cedar in the forest, whose head brushed the vault of the sky. From this wise elder, Enkidu crafted a cedar gate and dedicated it to Enlil. Then at the end of his life, Enkidu turns and curses it.

O wooden gate of the forest, listen.
You are inert lumber now thanks to my strong axe.
Still, hear me with the ear you have no longer,
the heart you had while you were a tree,
when I wanted your timber.
(Epic of Gilgamesh)

Having called the door insensible, he then delivers a diatribe to "witless" wood, to the gate as though it were still a cedar—not only a cedar, but one that would comprehend his anger. Enkidu unburdens himself: he hopes a future king will come to despise the gate and wishes he himself could tear it down right now, as he previously tore down the tree. He is glad he killed the cedar, but enraged that he must die, and wants the tree to feel his hurt. In Enkidu's mind, the noble cedar is dead yet still-vigorous; desired yet hated; passive yet capable of feeling; deaf yet still can hear. His ambivalence will spread through sacred groves like wildfire.

Some began to condemn goddess worship. Questions were asked. Was Asherah a deity, tree, or pole? Cults changed, and her groves were destroyed. Prophets called her image shameful and accused her worshippers of debasing themselves in green and sacred places under trees. When Gideon demolished a shaded altar of Baal, he disturbed not only the standing stones. He burned a sacrifice with the trees of the grove.

Time went on. Look at the landscape: sacred or not, trees fall to heat bathhouses, forges, kilns, and funeral pyres. Charcoal makers and miners erase whole forests around their work sites. Their axes, saws, and wedges sleep now in museums.

The first symbol for Inanna was a doorpost framing the entrance to a storehouse for sweet dates. In essence it was still a trunk. A sacred tree, its nymph, or a date palm goddess seemed mere poles to the unaware, frames for ritual activity on the altar. In the guise of a living tree, a plank, or carved wooden pole, the goddess remained in plain sight. A formulaic arch to shade prayer, feast, or sacrifice, garlanded but stripped and dead—to some eyes.

Denuded or veiled, in blossom or in bud, she remained the goddess with upraised arms.

The Huluppu Tree

In that time, that faraway time, young Inanna rested in a distant
pasture. She was dreaming of sacred marriage rituals to come,
delighting in the allure of her vulva.
(Inanna and Enki)

Somewhere nearby, all alone, there grew a sapling, a water-
loving willow. It shot up on the bank of the Euphrates, where
moisture nurtured its budding leaves. But sometimes the god
of wind buffeted it, and sometimes the river god flooded it.
Finally, a torrent completely uprooted the scruffy seedling.

That day Inanna, strolling riverside,
plucked up the bedraggled shoot,
placed it in her woven basket,
brought it to her tender garden,
and settled it in holy earth.
She nurtured it with care.
This was the huluppu tree.
(Gilgamesh, Enkidu, and the Netherworld)

On a throne of lions sits a vegetation goddess. Worshippers
greet her with uplifted arms. Spiral curls hang luxuriantly over
full breasts; she cradles a leafy palm branch clustered with
dates; and long stalks ending in buds spring from her shoulders.
Her throne and footstool are sprouting tree limbs. Countless
variations of this scene are found engraved on Mesopotamian
stone vessels, seals, and plaques.

The crescent moon hangs above, mirroring the horned headdresses
of her adoring goddess attendants. Tamarisk-waisted maidens
approach with dippers of water, displaying ripening fruit still on

49

the tree for the goddess to approve. As birds and ibexes look on, she offers them a living stem in return.
(Akkadian cylinder seal with vegetation deities)

The garden attendants are greeting Inanna as a vegetally vigorous goddess. She was known to be tender toward plants.

The lithe green tendril of Inanna's body manifests in diverse forms: warrior, high priestess, fertility deity, or bride. Standing on a pair of lions, bulls, or mythical monsters:

She polishes her weapon — then ties dainty sandals on her feet.
She arranges her javelins — then clasps on a necklace of tender rosebuds.
She wraps herself in fearsome beauty, shuddering to behold.
She establishes shrines that brim with festive music —
founds whole priesthoods — then rushes away to the foothills,
surging like water that sweeps away a dam.
(Hymns to Inanna)

Like all gods and goddesses, she easily contains her opposite. Her care for fertility is passionate and unsparing. When she went missing, all mating stumbled.

No bull followed a cow,
no stallion courted a mare,
young men loitered inside
and did not seek out any girls.
(Ishtar's Descent to the Netherworld)

Her presence on earth is necessary for the continuation of life. But her concern for the survival of the entire cosmos also makes her instinctively dangerous to anything that overruns its natural limits, including the burgeoning human species. She is the fecund source of sexual generativity, yet also the unsentimental mother of a litter she is willing to cull.

In the Mesopotamian story of the primeval Flood, gods in council made dry-eyed long-term provisions to control human populations through cyclical deluge, disease, famine, drought, and war. Inanna is one of the goddesses who performs these decimations. She declares:

I trample,
deprive,
perplex,
slay,
haul back on the bridle,
heap up skulls like piles of dust.
I do not relent.
(Hymns to Inanna)

If any human work has been constructed without reverence for natural order, she is willing to say:

Let the whole house collapse.
(Medea)

Her strength is primordial:

The scarf she tosses on her shoulders
once encircled collar bones
already brittle in distant days,
before heaven and earth ever parted,
when the underworld and world still turned on one hinge.
She swathes her limbs in a transparent garment
that rippled with the motion of antediluvian gods.
(Hymns to Inanna)

Her cloak is handed down from gods so archaic that they are

nascent with mud and slime from the abyss.

Inanna embodies tender lullabies and visceral drives. Strengthened by her journey below, emerging out of chaos, she lightly holds the reins of the beast called civilization.

When she descends, and surrenders her adornments one at a time, her ensemble sounds strikingly like those that have been found in Sumerian royal graves of Ur. Inanna also carries something unique: a stone seal engraved with a map of heaven and earth. This talisman was not surrendered at any of the netherworld checkpoints where she was commanded to disrobe. The object, though it gleams only in poetic description, may be a primeval artistic conception of the Earth as one organism. Millennia before the Gaia hypothesis, Inanna wears this design.

Outside of birthing and killing, what else was intricately carved into her talisman? Humans wanted human-focused things to be inscribed there: equipment to shore up and invigorate civilization, things we never wanted to live without. Inanna wore some of these elements in her costume too. As a collection, Sumerians called these necessary luxuries or luxurious necessities the *mes*.

This ensemble of assets arises from divine wisdom, encompasses all that is skillful, creative, and memorable, and permeates life with savor and sweetness. The *mes* are cultural forms that include all arts and crafts. And even some intrigues and impositions—that once surmounted make humankind wiser.

The assemblage of *mes* constituted an argument for the divine origin of kings since kingship was right there in the collection. A desired correspondence between powers above and powers below eventually led earthly kings to call their own administration *mes*. Acclaimed in poetry, this diverse assemblage of abstract and concrete elements included scepters, weapons, songs, harps, dance, prostitution, staying at home, traveling, taverns, sheepfolds, family life, hairdressing, colorful clothes, slander, and the art of sympathetic listening. Also, *katabasis*.

Imagine human life without that gear: dull.

But Enki could revoke the *mes* from humans. And more than that. After taking away these skills, thrills, obstacles, and advantages, he could even forbid humans to miss them.

Myths about the *mes* disappearing remind us that cultural implements, arts, and customs are not docile servants under our control. They could turn in our hands, revolt, and abandon us for good. One ancient axe head boasted an inscription that the man who hewed with it would never grow weary. But could it also manage the reverse? The master's tools might decide to dismantle the master's house one day, since they helped build it in the first place. How could we make mud bricks without a brickmold, or the memory of how to use one? Sing without songs? Fortunately, we didn't need to find out. After Enki took them away from us, Inanna got them back.

First, she got Enki drunk. As soon as he turned them over to her in an inebriated round of beer toasts, she escaped in the nick of time. However, he quickly sobered up and decided against his largesse. He sent out hordes to confiscate the boat of heaven with its cargo of priceless *mes*. Each time they attacked, however, Ninshubur came to the rescue. She repelled wave after wave of monstrous and mythical creatures from Inanna's sacred boat. Afterward, everyone wanted to hear what happened, so Ninshubur told the story:

Each time they clamped down on our boat,
I fought them off.
Fifty ghastly spell-growling priests seized our laden boat.
Fifty heavy-handed giants captured our overflowing ship.
Fifty sharp-toothed sea serpents dragged back our laboring craft.
Fifty semidivine canal guardians hauled back our boat as it quaked.
It was close every time.
But I flung them all back, saved the mes, and defended my queen.
(Inanna and Enki)

When Enki finally gives in, Inanna docks her brimming boat safely in Uruk. The divine gifts are distributed to the people, and revels spring up around the pier. Her arrival became a yearly festival that attuned participants to the rhythms of all of life. Now we could sing, flirt, show off, dance, and procreate again.

When Inanna won the drinking game, some of the *mes* she carried out of Enki's palace took the shape of feminine adornments. Once more we glimpse headdress, jewelry, gown, and cosmetics. There was also a surveying set: a lapis lazuli measuring rod and line. Just as Enki's (sober) word is usually his command, Inanna's apparel is often her power. As part of her regalia, in addition to the cosmic stone seal, Inanna carries this rod and line. She displays these accessories in art and myth to remind us that we only borrow art and technology from the gods.

This is especially true for surveying tools that carve out portions of earth and define the subtle art of land ownership. A property line or boundary marker is an imaginary device, easily erased by a goddess.

She flicks it away as lightly as a mother brushes a fly
from the cheek of her sweetly sleeping child.
(Iliad)

Where human surveyors might wish to draw straight lines and operate within them, vegetation gods like Inanna create organic curves: palm trunks swaying, marshland undulating, hips of hillsides draped in gowns of thyme.

A circular glade for dancing or a shimmering swathe of herbs is more like a boundary Inanna would make: an organic margin to protect exuberant life within. One of her favorite protected places, not far from the dock where she delivered the *mes*, was her orchard in Uruk.

Here she might glory in lettuce watered by desire, nap under a delicious apple tree, or delight in her lifegiving and pleasure-giving holy womb. For her, virginity itself was an enclosed garden, sheltered yet gated, infinitely renewable. Inanna entered gardens to rejoice in her own fecundity, and to nourish their fertility too. She plans a rendezvous with her divine consort in a garden, where their union is propagative and erotic:

Rise out of the glistening willow leaves,
my lover. I will pour out plants,
I will pour out grain,
I will pour out sweet nectar of allure.

Let me bring you honey.
You bring me sweet fruit to taste.
Rise and grow ripe in your furrow.
(Songs of Inanna and Dumuzi; Vigorously He Sprouted)

This enthusiastic vegetation deity is the propagative aspect of the goddess who saved the huluppu and tended the sapling's growth when it was barely clinging to life. When it matured, a serpent who heard no incantations made its lair in the roots. In the limbs above, the monstrous Anzu bird built a nest for his young. In between, Lilith the apostate made her house inside the trunk.

All three—serpent, Anzu, and Lilith—are startling portents to appear inside a properly brought-up tree. Suddenly we remember that this infested huluppu was born a feral seedling. The skin-sloughing snake is adept in subterranean mysteries of life and death. Lion-headed Anzu shreds the clouds with his talons to unleash storms. Enigmatic Lilith was a rebellious goddess or restless child-killing demon who challenged and rejected patriarchy. They make a striking trio of insurgents.

But even more surprising than their appearance in a cultivated garden, is what the beings are contending against. Inanna is developing ideas that she only hinted at before:

Will it be long?
In what season will the tree
bestow a wonder,
my first splendid wooden throne?
In what season will the tree
bestow a wonder,
my first sumptuous wooden bed?
(Gilgamesh, Enkidu, and the Netherworld)

She begins to eye the huluppu tree not as a suppliant, a shade tree for orchard interludes, or a living trunk to lean against in moments of delight, but as raw material. She wants the tree she has tended to supply her with *mes*. This intention of hers introduces a more hard-hearted motivation for tending the tree, that of valuation. Specifically, valuable huluppu furniture, bequeathed to her by the deceased tree. Now we realize why she cultivated the transplant while wondering out loud about a throne and bed. Now we know why Inanna was careful never to touch the tree with the intimacy of her bare hand. Harvesting the huluppu as a commodity will raise one priority (deploying status symbols) over another (the life of the tree).

As soon as the equation of tree with timber grows in Inanna's mind, the thought of Gilgamesh might enter ours. And in fact, at this very moment in the story, the hero strides into Inanna's enclosed and sacred garden. His axe is in his hand and his tree-felling companions in carpentry are by his side. The moment he heard of Inanna's distress he took up his Cedar Mountain axe. In successive blows, he exterminates the serpent, expels Anzu with his children to the mountain, and confronts Lilith, who demolishes her own house and escapes to the desert. He uproots the entire tree, and then his followers saw up the trunk and give the wood to Inanna for her throne and bed. From some scraps, Gilgamesh makes two objects for himself.

The wooden items must be dummy weapons or sports

equipment, because Gilgamesh and his companions become obsessed with playing with them. So, the huluppu has been made into social currency: status symbols and playthings. And perhaps the tree has even taken some revenge. Huluppu-wood sport turns deadly when Enkidu is trapped in the underworld, trying to retrieve the new equipment from a crack in the earth. As for the wooden bed, its slats will host proper domesticated sexual encounters that will not take place on earthy garden ground. Now we see why Lilith annihilated her house. She would not allow it to join the bedframe meant to fix Inanna's sexuality in place.

Instead, when the tree changed from a living organism into organic material, Lilith fled into the wild unknown.

As a mistress of dissidence, Lilith does not simply dart away. She breaks domestic bonds and escapes cultivation, for her life in the protected garden has been shattered by the price that cultivators exact. As an extravagantly fertile counterpart to Inanna, Lilith ends up unsheltered, far from civilization, and decisively not situated on a skillfully carpentered, huluppu-grained throne or bed. She runs amok.

To where? To places truly unknown? Some say she fled to the sea. Some say it was into the sort of places not frequented by city types, but intimately known to a goddess who spurned the arts of civilization: Ninhursag, mistress of regions we sometimes cunningly term wasteland. Her name meant "revered lady of stony ground." She loved to wander borderland all others found impassible and meet nobody on her path. On her brow the desert blossomed, and she clothed herself in foothills. She wept when wild animals wept. She is the reason why, after nature pretends to be tamed, it multiplies wildly once we are gone until no traces of domestication remain.

Lilith deemed it wise to abandon not only the garden, but beds, thrones, axes, heroes, and *mes* in general. Desolation was perfectly hospitable for her, the uninhabited perfectly habitable. Ninhursag is not a goddess of fertile cultivated fields or orchards, but a goddess of obstinate rock. Both goddesses are wellsprings of productivity and fertility, but each in her own way, on her own uncultivated terms.

The young of ravening beasts are in her tender care.
(Agamemnon)

Ninhursag and the snake-bird-rebel trio in the huluppu remind us that ravening beasts follow inscrutable destinies of their own. Their escapes from heroic control are carved into the stone seal of the cosmos.

The huluppu tree fell because Inanna brought Gilgamesh into her garden to turn the tree she rescued into wood. Beyond even that, Inanna brought the hero into her garden to rescue her. She entreats him quite pitifully to fix her tree. The goddess of infinite moods appears here in a new role: damsel in distress.

Axe-wielding Gilgamesh is a guest in her story. But he walks on stage with powerful impact, flanked by his entourage and cloaked in the symbolism of mastery wherever he steps. We know him as an ogre-slayer and monument-maker from his epic. Gilgamesh also belongs to a cadre of brawny heroes idealized in Mesopotamian art. We see a beast-master in action:

Lapis forehead groomed in ebony curls,
nude but for the warrior-belt at his waist,
he wrestles to a standstill two rearing ivory bulls,
or plants his foot on the spine of a grimacing lion.
The rampant beasts are muscled, maned,
curls groomed on their foreheads. Necks in his grip,
their bearded faces look out at us, exactly like his own.
(The Great Lyre of Ur)

Once the huluppu tree got out of hand and into Gilgamesh's grip, did its nature need containment to ensure survival? Whose need? Whose survival? A domesticated version of Inanna is happy that this bearded and belted Gilgamesh has come into her garden and brought his beast-master skills along. He will master the tree that is now perceived as infested, chaotic, and uncivilized, with his taming and domesticating *mes*. In the grip of kingly arrogance and aggression, he will overturn the unyielding, even if the savagery he grasps is mirrored by his own.

Who is this helpless goddess who summoned him? She is shrouded in contradiction. Inanna, standing in her own garden, is demoted to a docile sidekick. What happened to her vegetal power, her tender care for plants? Why is she eager for goods from the huluppu tree?

Inanna does wear the stone seal of heaven and earth, and she does carry with her the beauteous *mes*, even to the seven gates. In the *Epic of Gilgamesh,* she boasts that she can heap storehouses with harvest or send famine. Not all organisms are destined to reach maturity, and humans need materials to survive, resources like huluppu or boxwood. The word "resource" views trees as Inanna came to value huluppu, and as Gilgamesh valued cedar.

The prehistoric mistress of animals nursed young wild creatures, yet she also helped hunters—within strict limits. She was a conservationist hunter who delighted in the chase, the two- or four-footed predator ready to thin the herbivore herd. Or was she? Motives cloaked in myth are ambiguous, the better to awaken curiosity and reflection. Maybe young seedlings shaded by the huluppu's growth needed sunlight. Maybe Inanna appears here as a damsel in distress because her worship was waning in the face of jealous gods. Maybe the myth portrays a tree raised in a temple precinct, destined for cultic furniture all along. Or maybe Inanna mirrors a dynastic queen, in need of a fine throne for rule and a fine bed for conception of royal heirs.

In our largely human-specific law codes, we have developed terms like fratricide, patricide, infanticide, or matricide, to speak of close killing. We think of human lovers, or parents with nursing infants, entwining close enough to breathe one another's breath. Are plants more distant than this? We breathe their outbreath with every breath. Who is more intimate with us? We have no common term for dendrocide. Yet in synchrony we breathe together with plants to breathe at all. The consequences of dendrocide are grave, but they are also silent, invisible, and slow. They are so archaic that they wear primordial robes, and we pretend they do not exist, or we hope they do not know what we are up to. The constant resuscitation that plants perform on us is invisible, but in every single moment, it is all that fills our lungs.

Who is alive in the life of a tree? A trio of wildings? A goddess whose life is coextensive with the tree? Cellulose, xylem, and phloem? When Inanna imports timber calculation into her sacred garden, she choked its soil with valuation customs. The buds and branches sprouting from her shoulders take on new meaning. Her date palm attendants draw back. She stands a guest, an outsider in her own orchard. Lost in her own myth. Or maybe she abandoned this myth. I wonder if, like her shadow Lilith, she has broken down her house and escaped to the wilderness, but the story covers up her tracks. As in a dream, we see her standing in the garden beside Gilgamesh, but somehow, within the enclosure, Inanna is nowhere to be found.

Animate and Inanimate

*The wood thrush has a complex throat that allows it to sing two
notes at the same time and harmonize with its own voice.*

Ancient poets of Sumer composed in more than one dialect, and
the dialects were gendered. Sounds written for performance
by a female voice could appear in *Emesal*, "delicate" or "thin
tongue." For example, in *Inanna's Descent* when a god or the
(male) narrator speaks they use one dialect; when a goddess
speaks, her words are in another mode. Noticing the difference
between their tongues was a breakthrough that led to the
decipherment of broken clay tablets that had long laid separated
in museums across the world. I wonder how artists performed
the voices when poetry was sung.

The score of musical Sumerian speech expands still further.
"Wood" had its own symbol in Sumerian, distinguishing it
from other raw materials or swaying trees. Signs expressed the
difference between what is animate, inanimate, and intensely
animate, in other words, divine.

Intensely alive clay tablets on museum shelves burrow between
Mesopotamian stone seals and terra cotta plaques, bearing nature
symbols everywhere. We find compassion, delight, and danger
in them: sea-Nammu, storm-Enlil, date-palm-Inanna. Bird men
on trial before bull-helmeted gods. Feather-skirted goddesses
brandishing clusters of heavy fruit. Out of their shoulders leap
lightning, grain, sunrays, and fishy streams.

Humbaba radiates *melam*, the vigor of being intensely alive,
and Inanna radiates date palm blossoms, arrows, or bolts of
energy from her shoulders. The symbol for divinity looked like
a star. It radiated the vigor of uniquely dynamic forms of life.

Look deep into life forms and see shimmering, pulsating cell
membranes, the ceremonial fringed dancing-capes of being.

Long before we saw a cell shimmer under a microscope, we saw life shimmer in myth.

If we started to speak like this, our words would scintillate. They might transform to sound alive, or not. The same words might bear signs to distinguish living and nonliving. Grain in the field vs. grain in the storehouse. Land under asphalt vs. lifegiving land. A taxidermy thrush in a glass case vs. a thrush who alights on a willow. Tools in the field breaking up soil might become animate to debate each other about who was most sturdy and useful. Sheep might contest grain, or heron argue with turtle. Sumerians did compose such dialogues.

They also poured sacrificial oil on sacred stones and sacred heads crafted from stone, wood, or clay, believing that the image would savor luxury and fragrance. In the Flood story, lean gods need human adoration to survive, and grow hungry for human offerings.

We think of the singer's lyre, and the bow of life or death. Language is a lyre that can drip honeyed words or shed biting arrows. Sacred statues were torn down when sacred groves were felled, and bloody conflicts raged over how living icons were or were not. It has sometimes been believed necessary, to smash or saw down something, first to conceive of it as an object, unliving, or weirdly alive.

Tree or timber, pig or pork, Humbaba's head on his neck or as a trophy in a bag.

Statues were intriguing cases, leading lives that spiraled between categories: sometimes animate, sometimes inanimate, like a cedar gate or boxwood goddess. Cult statues were not made simply from stone or wood. The material was carefully chosen and shaped by prayerful hands. Once a sculpture was ritually brought to life, it lived as a god. It accepted or rejected offerings, traveled to festivals, bathed, banqueted, listened to music, and changed ensembles of clothing. The image might consent only to be seen—or be safe to be seen—by select personnel at limited times; it might stay single or get married. Devotional ceremonies of washing the mouth and opening the mouth with living water brought to life the sculpture's awareness. Only then would the image no longer be called an image, but be called Inanna, Enki, or Ninhursag.

Without devotion, a sculpture did not feel or think. Or hear prayers, or respond to human needs. The difference lay in how the statue was cared for. This was as true in historical processions as it was in Homeric poetry.

> Go as queen to the temple of the goddess who protects the citadel,
> gathering around you a throng of women in high esteem,
> and solemnly carry gifts to be sacrificed.
> Take a fragrant robe; choose the palace's most luxurious,
> one that lies hidden in the innermost chamber,
> one that shines like a star, elaborate embroidery of many hands,
> by far your most graceful handiwork of weaving.
> Lay this as an offering on the knees of lovely-haired Athena.
> (Iliad)

On that day, Athena refused the offering and averted her face from the queen. After his friend's death, Gilgamesh tried to comfort himself with a statue of Enkidu, but it didn't work. The decline of the wood thrush, rarely seen now near the Cuyahoga, began with an averted face.

We saw Inanna in the underworld when her cult image — and therefore she herself — stood in peril of turning into tarnished metal and sawn-up wood that was unalive. When our tongues say Athena or wood thrush, are they as alive as we are? Less alive? More alive? Does the difference resonate, coiled inside our devotion?

Helix

Uncoiling a strand of woodbine near the cattail marsh. Sometimes unwinding from the base, sometimes in a descending spiral. Rather than tug, gently uncurl. At last, the beech sapling springs free.

Inanna's cascading tresses and shoulder-sprouting tendrils were springy spirals, vibrant with the shimmering of eros. Her energy is a coiled spring, superabundantly alive. Ancient words and signs for radiance had meanings that leapt from luminous to brilliant, from dazzlingly godlike to divine. These image-fronds curl to clasp the rippling animation of heroes and form the archaic name of Zeus.

A shimmer evokes wonder wherever it appears: apple leaves dappling the breeze, the vibrating voice of lyre strings, the multihued procession to a temple, or a cuttlefish pulsing with undulating waves of color, unsure whether to mate.

When Zeus mates with Hera, goddess of the hour of ripening, dewy vegetation springs up all around.

He enfolded his wife in his arms, and
at their embrace the earth burst into fresh budding green:
a bed of grass, juicy clover, crocus, and hyacinth bouquets,
so luxurious, they were cushioned far from the ground.
They lay down together and draped themselves in a lovely golden cloud—
dew overflowed, glistening.
(Iliad)

When Inanna bathes, dresses, and opens her door to greet her lover, she shines radiant as the moon. When she appears as the morning and evening star, she illuminates joyful desire.

Let the man come to me, let him come to my chamber.
Let in the brilliant bridal procession.
(A Song of Inanna and Dumuzi)

Her rites were associated with dance: playful, exuberant frolics that invited her worshippers to be swept up into her intimate, instinctual appeal. A procession for Inanna enveloped celebrants in gorgeous aromas, sights, sounds, and colors.

It is a day for flute, kettledrum, tambourine, and harp,
hairdressers, costumers, acrobats, and brewers.
At the new moon greet her with a whirling dance!
What are you waiting for?
Put a ribbon in your hair, tilt a mask over your face, and come.
Incense already rises, oils waft perfumes, rich banquets bask.
Pour beer for her, bake cakes for her,
bring honey, cheese, butter, dates, and wine—your best!
(Inanna and Iddin-Dagan)

Thrilling dance, vegetal vitality, and the rhythms of sexual impulse cannot be commanded, any more than she can. All gods were volatile, but unpredictability is the heart of Inanna. Her vivacity is the sexual vitality she bestows on all that lives.

We know that in changing all things find repose. To play with some variations Heraclitus may or may not have had in mind, maybe in fluctuation—spontaneity, erotic glances, the edge of surrender and pulsation of play—all things repose.

Continual flux: we may tremble before it.

Some things are admittedly more changeable than others. There were deities of the female sexual response, genital-goddesses, who assisted Inanna. Their names hint at subtleties no longer understood. Are they early words who have already rebelled to throw off the yoke of meaning? They faded into obscure "private parts" when domesticated reproduction espoused a fundamental need for predictability, but no particular use for female pleasure. Perhaps such pleasure moved around too much. As Lucretius advised Roman husbands:

> *Surely our wives have no need to make movements, as prostitutes do, in bed.*
> *Lascivious motions divert the plow from its furrow.*
> (The Nature of Things)

When female anatomy escaped from proper speech, the new modesty dealt out doses of cultural amnesia. A woman wise in the ways of arousal, a goddess delighting in her vulva, became females not to be trusted. But forgetfulness of mythic truth is delicate, dangerous business. When Gilgamesh obliterated the mysterious Stone Ones on his quest, he did not realize they were vital to his search for wisdom. He learned their significance too late when they lay smashed around his feet. This was after he had gone berserk in a big game hunting spree, killing lions, panthers, cheetahs, tigers, leopards, and other carnivores. No wonder Siduri, the tavern keeper at world's edge, bolts her door and hides when she sees him coming. He threatens to splinter it down. The mythic gardener Shukaletuda tore up every plant in his care, refused to water anything, and assaulted the sleeping Inanna. Afterward he wept and complained that the land had turned to dust.

Where have our goddess-words for genitals gone? To dust? Have we wept for them?

They did leave plentiful clues behind, some in anatomy, some in the upper air. One clue to their disappearance can be found in the bold claim an ancient philosopher made about a goddess of light. She is Iris, divine messenger of the gods, who gave us the word iridescent. She leapt from Mount Olympus in multihued curves across the sky. Here is what he said:

The goddess Iris is a cloud of colors.
(Xenophanes)

This does not seem momentous. He went on for a few words. The cloud is "a thing that is purple, red, and yellowish-green." His early way of describing a light spectrum fits with early philosophy, full of curiosity about the nature of nature. Someone was going to go first to try to demystify the rainbow; Xenophanes looked up at the sky and did it. Before his innovative scrutiny, wind-footed Iris glistened. She could even enter and exit the underworld with confidence, using her gentle hands to part dreams, like cobwebs that hid her way. She dove through the upper air with panache.

She positioned her veil of a thousand hues, poised on her toes,
and traced a curving arc across heaven with her gliding leap.
(Metamorphoses)

As a multihued thing, however, Iris enters a new story, demythologized one sheer shimmer at a time at the gates of sober scrutiny. This new dialect, that objectifies the divine, isolates humanity in a cosmos that used to teem with gods, all with colorful stories of their own. When Iris still leapt free, she incandesced the atmosphere with rain-drenched sun and rainbows. Pinned like a dragonfly in a case, however, she is suddenly analyzable, collected in a herd of atmospheric phenomena, where Zeus (thunder), Helios (sun) and Selene (moon) will soon stand bare and shivering too.

In Xenophanes' formulation, Iris has taken an unexpected turn. For starters, she has leapt down from Mount Olympus in a manner that seems...unerotic.

Where is the *hili* in that?

When fruit trees gleam with ripeness, when Inanna is ready for a date, or when cult personnel dance, they exude *hili*: a

Sumerian word for sparkling charm and sexual allure. Someone who is irresistibly attractive exudes it. As the embodiment of sexuality for her people, Inanna generates it on a cosmic scale. So do parades in multicolored costumes to the accompaniment of ecstatic festival music—all sensual pleasure, bathed in a charismatic glow. In the give and take of *hili*, something desirable positively radiated desire.

Spring.
Dripping quinces,
swollen streams,
shy nymphs,
secret gardens.

Grapes ripen,
vines tendril a little tighter.
As they entwine,
I shake with love.
(Ibycus)

Though the ancient lyric poet Praxilla was ridiculed for finding the dusky sheen of vegetables and fruit equally longed-for as the stars and moon, the *hili* of grape tendril is what she meant. All music, all lyric poets holding lyres rely on coiled tension in strings. Then comes that moment when the lyre's pure voice sings songs of war, when the warrior's plucked bow sounds a note that makes him long for peace.

From cell membranes to provocative allure, to waves on water, to cedars shedding wind, to the voice rising and falling to sing, to the twists and turns of a myth well told, all of life shimmers. And scintillation was Iris's domain.

To tell the truth, everyone realized in the beginning that Iris was a cloud of colors. The knowledge canceled no festivals because Xenophanes's news was nothing new. They also remembered that Iris's father was a god named Thaumas, "sacred wonder." The only problem with the cloud idea lies in its habitual reading as a stilling, chilling exclusivity: when Iris is *nothing more* than a spectrum of colors. When the rainbow is only a piece of weather, cells stiffen, dew dries away, and *hili* dancers halt mid-step.

We do well to remember that on an errand of anger, Iris could obscure her face too.

Storm-footed, thunder swirling at the hem of her gown,
Iris leapt from the heavens and plummeted straight into the steel-grey ocean.
Over her head the night water barely rippled, groaning in lament.
(Iliad)

We met divine radiance in *melam*, a stupefying power. And still today, we call some faces striking or stunning, and tell brides they are radiant. There is no way to pin the erotic down. Eros and Aphrodite were hailed as unconquered and unconquerable, even when only at play. What else shimmers strikingly? For one thing, a Neolithic girl's coming-of-age fringed skirt, perfect for a come-hither swishing dance. For another thing, a Paleolithic goddess's fertility belt of string. And Aphrodite's glimmering sash, for another.

She lends it only rarely, with instructions to seduce:

Take this sash and wear it between your breasts, tuck it in beneath your gown.
It glistens with intricate designs, embroidered diagrams of heaven and earth.
There — like so. Its charm is irresistible. Now whatever you desire will not be undone.
(Iliad)

Myth exchanges Inanna's stone seal for the linen band of Aphrodite, and deftly folds it in the bosom of the goddess of sex-appeal. Its embroidered schemas reveal and conceal all of creation. Earth wove it long ago, with no need for skein or pattern, only threads of longing and wonder. Aphrodite wears her design.

Daybreak in a world of *hili* was not sunrise. Look east: it was the sprint of the sun-god's chariot drawn by fiery steeds; it was the epiphany of Aurora, the goddess of dawn, rosy-fingered, saffron-robed, rising from the bed of her beloved to her golden throne. Is she an enchanted archetype, a natural phenomenon, or senseless matter? We celebrated the helix in mythic tongues before we learned any genetics. The spiral shoots of the ancient word *helix* already encircled the shimmering that permeates vibrant life, the dynamics of union and division, and the procreation of all compelling attractions. Look up at a rainbow's curve and witness the dawn of an ancient dilemma.

Is Iris an epiphany? That is the crux, the convoluted question.

He Filled the Tigris

The god of civilizing wisdom and domesticating fertility does not find his task convoluted. He mounts the Tigris, and as the river begins to flow, the practice of irrigation is born.

Like a bull father Enki rears up,
lifts his phallus, ejaculates —
he fills the Tigris with fresh water.
(Enki and the World Order)

This is Enki. When we last saw him, he was delving into subterranean elements, plunging through the Apsu to the underworld, or penetrating earth to establish a temple. Now he creates a river on dry land.

The ambition to control whole bodies of water is ancient. In history, kingdoms fell when inimical kings diverted rivers. In legend, waterworks prepared a lavish burial complex, when engineers diverted an entire river to make a grave for the hero Gilgamesh. Laborers dug a new channel for the Euphrates River, constructed his tomb on the riverbed, laid his prized possessions and personnel inside, then released the flood. His tomb sank below the current and disappeared forever.

Something is articulated here about the animate landscape and humanity's place in it. What form will that relationship take?

River gods surfaced in Greece as men whose beards gushed water, as bulls, or bull-men, guarding river fords or swimming. Live bulls could be sacrificed in rivers or the sea. Some maidens said a river god had taken, or tried to take, their virginity when they waded into the water. We know that cults flourished around rivers and riverbanks. Lusty Enki and the Tigris may flow beneath later river-bull-god myths.

In the days of the earliest recorded stories, human subsistence was precarious. Small scale horticulture sustained small households. A natural brake on human nutrition and reproduction acted wherever there was "too much" water (marshes) or "too little" water (desert). But to the gods' dismay, humans began to engulf the earth with their clamor, and raise a tumult with ever-increasing hordes, and a significant increase in population became a mortal achievement. A larger labor force made crews for farming that served new irrigation-intensive grain monocultures. This was the dawn of large scale agriculture in an arid land.

Marshland is a far cry from desert cut by irrigation ditches. How to bridge the distance? Already at the dawn of myth, concerns arose that the ever-expanding pursuit and abduction of water endangered earth and plants, who thrived luxuriantly near marshes, riverbanks, and springs. We recall Enki, Nammu, Apsu, and Tiamat, and remember that wetland suggested both sexual activity and conflict. If we focus on plow and bull alone, we risk losing sight of a different essential truth: the fertile garden and body of Inanna, filled with watered and water-loving life. In arid climates, moist ground fringed with soft plants suggested pleasure and mythical mating. But certain Mesopotamian, Greek, and Roman gods and heroes prowled the vegetation of riverbanks, shores, springs, and wells. Locales on the edge of water became classically perilous places for girls and goddesses. Like Enki's penetration of the depths with his boat, not all mating was consensual. Introducing water into land that was naturally dry was troubled from the beginning.

Enki was lauded as lord of sweet water.

Eloquent and wise,
prolific source of decrees,
the one whose word rings true.
Artful at incantations,

catalyst for wide destinies,
ambidextrous with sleight of words.
(Enki and the World Order)

Even on their own, words are wise, far-reaching, protean tools who know things, including how to twist on the tongue. Crafty Enki is a trickster, a protean god of mischief and cunning. He does not rely on brute force, but brandishes winning words.

When Enki supplanted the goddess Ninhursag to become third in the Sumerian pantheon of gods, his promotion made the most-worshipped triad all males. We will see how she felt about that directly. He is associated not only with deep fresh water, but also water that is in use: diverted, channeled water, even the Great Flood meant to eradicate human life. He is the one who helped humankind survive the inundation; he is the one who helped Ninshubur rescue Inanna. He is a formidable benefactor—and a doubtful and dangerous one. Enki's commands are daunting, especially when his words are disguised. He is a god of riddles, not solutions.

Here is a riddle, one that takes us back to the marshes.

From the marshland Enki reaches out.
As he stretches out his phallus,
ditches overflow with semen,
reed beds are parted,
and he spills into the waterways.
(Enki and Ninhursag)

As he unabashedly stretches or reaches out with his phallus, in the marshes he mounts the mistress of wilderness Ninhursag, whom he had eclipsed in Sumerian cult. This is the first scene in a sequence where Enki, the god who fills rivers and irrigation ditches, "overflows" into four generations of Ninhursag and female descendants. One after another conceives.

When Ninhursag acts to counter him, the mythic pattern ends. She wipes the semen from his great-granddaughter's body and plants it in the ground; there spring up eight novel plants. But the god of wisdom—a clever title for a clever god— seeks to control the plants too. They disturb him, appearing outside his understanding. Even more perplexing, he who knows all words does not know their names. Enki's ignorance matters because ancient naming was a tool for mastery over the natural world. Or attempted mastery. In agriculture and animal husbandry, labeling and categorizing constituted semi-magical semantic dominations useful for taming the landscape and living organisms, including plants. Named goddesses Enki impregnated, but he is stymied by anonymous seedlings. As a solution, he asks his right-hand-man to name them, and one by one, as they are classified, he tears them up and eats them, seeking to comprehend their destinies.

But eating the mystery plants has toxic consequences. When he consumes the eight young beings, Ninhursag's rage is finally felt. She and the sprouts conspire together to make him dreadfully sick. In the end, when he is close to death, at the beseeching of all the gods, she is finally induced to heal him, and the trickster's appetite escapes consequence one more time. For the moment.

The transition from the self-fertilizing water goddess Nammu to daughterly deities who produce vegetation when they are mounted may reflect Neolithic to Bronze Age innovations. These changes included not only new water channeling techniques, and the expansion of urban centers further into their environs, but also the transition from female-centered horticulture to male-centered agriculture, exchanging the light hoe for the more penetrating plow. Within the story, yet somehow removed from it, stand the eight intriguing plants, seedlings who are poisonous only to those who disrespect their vulnerability, self-determination, and growth. Enki commanded goddesses to lie down. But the new plants resist his plans, and spoil further consumption, via their delivery of a natural consequence: sickness. In this way tender seedlings heal Enki's cycle of violence. The one who harvests brutally, prematurely, or indiscriminately weakens his own life.

With Enki, the Tigris, and Ninhursag, ancient anxieties about laying ax to tree or driving pickax into earth are joined by myths that express misgivings about canals, drains, dikes, and dams. It was understood that Enki's phallus pushed freshwater where it would never again run free. As time passed, control and "improvement" of natural flows through tunnels, pipes, and aqueducts converted water into a public utility, in ever more elaborate buildings to channel natural springs.

In late antiquity, Apollo revealed a final oracle from Delphi, the last that would ever be heard.

Gone is the laurel,
gone is the voice of the prophetic spring.
The water that spoke is silent.
(Kedrenos)

Looking out over the Tigris or Cuyahoga River, a broad and varied panorama unfolds. Bull gods, eight plants, and the springtime promise of tender lettuce. Turning our hand to plow or sluice gate, we feel the eye of Enki. We work for water— disappearing, tainted, rising water—in ways never dreamed before.

One Sumerian way of describing impending death for a person was to say that their floodwaters were beginning to rise.

In the beginning, it was not a god of vegetation, a goddess of grain, or a date palm maiden who taught us how to irrigate, but a god who devises conundrums for others to solve. Preying on goddesses, devouring seedlings, and intensive irrigation end with sickness in the stomach, and drought when water fails.

Crops crumble into dust, and where there once was water stalks thirst.

In my mind's eye, there stoops Tantalus, the archetypal devourer. Once he thirsted to deceive the gods; now he is trapped in the underworld of the *Odyssey*. He cannot reach water to quench his thirst no matter how hard he tries.

He stood in parched and painful torment,
in a pool that lapped at his neck, almost up to his chin.
Raving with thirst, he tried to drink, but captured nothing.
Every time the old man crouched over, mouth dirt-dry from drought,
every drop of water was gulped down by the ground.
It sank away and disappeared in ripples of dust around his feet.
The ground cracked where he stood, dried by divine revenge.
(Odyssey)

But Enki always has water; it is his very element. And his resumé is artful: trickster of freshwater deeps, plunger into the Absu, stretcher into the marshes, diverter of water to where appetites want it to run. His potency was a fearsome river in flood.

The bull of the Tigris delved into soil and tore noble loincloths to transform the landscape and its vegetation. His myths have brought curiosities to light: plants who pronounce their own destinies and resist consumption; empathy for vegetation goddesses and the wild water they love.

I look at the Cuyahoga River and wonder with the Sumerian poet, "Where is it sung?"

Lympha

Water calmed as the goddess raised her face from the pool. Sprinkling her forehead with crystalline drops as she drew moist tresses over her shoulder, she began her story.
(Metamorphoses)

The Roman goddess Lympha, robed in limpid undulations, appears and disappears according to rhythms invisible on the surface. In cult, she is the personified life of water running free. Although Sumerians could use the divine or animate sign for water even when it was channeled into canals or pools, from the perspective of classical antiquity, Lympha dwelt only in water that was pure, clear, and finding its own way, emerging from a natural spring. Such water was called living water. If any of those features were absent, then so was she.

Local nymphs, sinuous spirits, dwelt in springs, inseparable from the landscape. Basins did not contain her living essence but did whisper of their pristine source; they remembered her and provided her reflection for worshippers inside temple precincts. Dipped from the wild, vessels of holy water graced the entrance of ancient sanctuaries to cleanse those who would enter holy ground. Everyone who entered trailed fingers in the clear water and sprinkled themselves, or scattered drops around themselves in a circle.

When water was caught, a liquid rather than a nymph remained. But here is a delight: gathering of water was women's work. The girl with a vessel of water on her head appears frequently in art from excavated sacred sites. Archaic poets likened jars to wombs; the first woman arrives in Greek myth carrying one filled with sorrow and hope. Lympha attends the woman walking with a vessel to the spring, then home to house or home to sanctuary, in a veiled dance of slow time. Fluid in clay jars, once delivered home, quenched thirst, though it was a step removed from the fortunate woman's hand that had dipped into the cool upswell.

The daily visit to the scenic native spring was a duty, a pleasure, and a lingering moment for reflection and ritual contact with the ever-flowing feminine divine. In a living fountain, leaning over the water, she could see a rippling unformed face she could not see anywhere else.

Water can always shift course, sink away, or surge up in an unexpected place. In her gushing gown of freshets, any water nymph might make an epiphany. Then when she spilled away, wanderers were left wondering whether they had spotted her or not.

He recognized her faintly, or thought he had...
like someone who, when the moon is young,
glimpses, or imagines for a moment he had seen
a pale new crescent rising through the clouds.
(Aeneid)

To invite the epiphany of evanescent Lympha, shelters for her presence were created. A nymphaeum or shrine to the nymphs could be a cave, spring, or grove in natural form. With some careful chiseling here and there, a rock spring became a rustic basin for offerings, with garlands, figurines, and marble plaques arranged above. Women tied ribbons of homemade cloth on overhanging branches, and shepherds hung up goat-milk buckets and whittled flutes. The place had healing powers. Nymphaea survived in remote areas until late antiquity, when some found new use as Christian shrines; until then, Lympha and her relatives thrived in art, myth, cult, and private prayer. As descendants of primeval Oceanus all seas, lakes, and waterfalls were kin. From whitewater rapid to rivulet, together they make a vivid pageant when all the waters on earth assemble in the halls of Olympus before Zeus.

Devotees affirmed their bond with nymph-haunted nature with material offerings, and with patient work of their hands: daily caretaking of springs, shrines, and gardens. Who were these custodians?

Lifegiving and benevolent as they were, sometimes nymphs abducted those they loved. A man who encountered them face to face might became a nympholept, someone "taken hold of" by nymphs. This sacred possession or awakening was *enthousiasmos*, the word behind all our enthusiasms. Being taken by nymphs brought gifts of inspiration, and the nympholept expressed visions through carving, painting, poetry, and prophecy. Like a woman who tends one cherished roadside shrine in the rural Mediterranean of today, an archaic devotee lived out a steadfast commitment. He might become a hermit, his life focused on intimate rituals. Ancient evidence survives for a handful of men who dedicated their lives to the worship of nymphs in a cave.

Archedamos of Thera was a nympholept in ancient days who lived alone as he cherished a cave near Vari in Greece. He left messages in stone to say that he was taken and directed to perform his life's work there. What lured him rapt to this wild shrine? Was this the work of Lympha and the eros of nymphs?

O loveliest of rivers, you surge to meet
wine-blue waters of the sea,
and as you say farewell to land,
you relax, and flow out languidly
to end your turbulent voyage in peace.

Playful young girls come thronging,
rinsing tender bodies with delicate hands,
as if some healing enchantment
flowed in your gentle waters.
(Alcaeus)

What is the eros of nymphs? Not anything to be defined. The mythical hero Odysseus disappeared for years with the shining nymph Kalypso in her poplar-shadowed, cedar-scented, sensually landscaped spring-watered garden and cave, when he was supposed to be heading home. Sumerian love poems are romantic and suggestive; earthy would be a perfect word for unions they describe. Early Greek romances hint at sexual discovery, entice with erotic language, but never display too much. The ancient novel *Daphis and Chloe* tells a story of sacred sensual awakening, centered around a pastoral grotto the innocent lovers tend together, sacred to the nymphs of the place.

Following his own mystical path, Archedamos fell under the spell of a place where goddesses spoke, city voices grew dim, and trickling water inspired divine communion. For many years, likely for the rest of his life, he devoted himself to Vari Cave, and cultivated fruit trees, herbs, and flowers near the entrance. He carved votive inscriptions and sculptures, including a self-portrait holding his tools. An amateur artist and immigrant, his rough inscriptions include the sayings:

Archedamos the Theran, a nympholept, instructed by the Nymphs, worked on this cave

and

Archedamos the Theran grew a garden for the Nymphs.

His devotion to living water transformed the work of his calloused hands into poetic and cultic offerings. He probably supported himself by weaving willow wreaths, molding simple votives, or accepting offerings from pilgrims. He became a marginal person, a mystic figure dwelling on the borderland, away from the secular world.

Such men did not live only in ancient days. Distant follower of such visionaries, there was a marginal stone carver, an untrained artist who was enchanted into isolation, who lived in a forested watershed near the Cuyahoga Valley of the last century.

Hidden in a dense stand of beech overlooking a lake to the west, wandering among sandstone ledges threaded with hemlock, I suddenly come face to face with a monumental carved sphinx, who crouches with her flanks only partially unembedded from the cliff, her paws shedding fern. She guards the obscure artworks of a bricklayer and aspiring sculptor, carvings that became the life's work of a man ancient Greeks would have thought a nympholept. His choice of bride—a woman who left her homestead only for church and died a year after the wedding—unsettled her family and he became an outcast, working with his tools in the forest behind the old house. In the years after her death, he spent his days here, crawled on sandstone cliffs and carved. Did he have two misunderstood loves: his lost bride, and these shadowy stones?

We have no modern framework for understanding him that fits as kindly or as gently as discarded ancient ones do: nympholepsy and *enthousiasmos*.

Drifting up from the forest floor, his enigmatic carvings swim upward from rippling rock formations originally carved by ocean. Moss-encrusted visages with brows of gnarled stone reveal the peculiar aliveness of cliff faces. Layers of fern, lichen and moss spill over symbols that peer out dreamlike from the shadowy narrow rock walls in silence. The crucified Christ, a family patriarch, and the Sphinx all look out from faces flat like moons, like hammered Helladic death masks. Beech roots tangle, framing the foreheads with hair. Hidden among and beneath overhanging precipices, echoing cries of jay and hawk, these were never meant for a museum; perhaps never even meant to be seen. They are private devotions to nymphs of beech and stone.

When it was rediscovered by modern explorers, the ancient

81

cave of Vari was screened by a fig tree whose branches shielded the entrance. The fig's water-seeking roots were visible three meters beneath the entrance, twining down beside handmade curving steps, finally emerging out on a stone shelf that Archedamos shaped for votive offerings.

Thousands of years later across the world, the twentieth-century devotee engraved religion, ancient mythology, and the name of the woman he loved into root-snaked rock. In two places on the sandstone, he engraved the simple words *IS ALL*.

I stand in the cold, looking down at the "is all" inscription that he etched for the recumbent stone Christ, whose outstretched left hand was almost touching a ruined outhouse of later date. The last time I hiked here the weathered grey slats were gone. It had been torn down. The old house has been leveled; other sculptures that once stood in the wooded border have been spirited away. Only Jesus surrounded by dry weeds, and a dilapidated gap-toothed barn remain. In this time of winter, when trees are bare, the site looks out over a distant lake. In summer, this open-air sanctuary is screened by rangy maples. In every rain and thaw, the layers seep. Everywhere around the lake stand markers for bridle trails and footpaths. Here there is no sign.

Archedamos and the twentieth-century carver, thousands of years apart, abandoned what is sometimes called the mainstream to dwell beside streams as hermits. To live out devotion in stone and honor places of prehistoric waters. Both men were captured and blessed by hidden recesses in the earth.

In the bodies of all nympholepts and all of us, two rivers wind: dark blood, and lustrous lymph. The goddess gave the translucent one its name, or someone borrowed it from her long ago. Inner lymph washes clean by flowing, and so did she. Indweller and protector of purifying springs, she aided the sick, the lost, or those who were sick with grief, for her fluid had the holy power to heal. For the psyche in need of return, for tree sap, for human lymph, the blocked stream finds her way through to new life.

Living water is powerful to make the choice to bless.

Never cross shining currents of ever-flowing rivers
before you cleanse your hands in the shimmering surface
and pray, contemplating the bright and lovely stream.
(Works and Days)

When the cave of Vari became a Christian shrine, excavators note that destruction of votive offerings, especially sculptural heads, seems to have been purposefully done. At the time of transition, the nymph shrine's votives were thrown broken into a heap and buried at the back of the cavern. In other locations, such burials look protective, with careful placement of nymph-holy things still whole, hidden in the earth. Was this meant to be until someone returned for them, after the hiding days? In the sacred landscape, the rustic secrecy of caves allowed humble, local nymph devotions to endure, and transform more gradually in history than monumental polytheisms that were publicly declared in temple architecture. While temples stood and fell, every cave echoed its own quiet and secret layers.

What Lympha is gracious to wash away, becomes cleansed detritus that is never coming back. If anyone thought of it in the future, ever more rarely and faintly, it would be the image of it dissolving, swept out in the current, gone. The woman at the well asked Jesus where living water could be found. The answer was standing right in front of her, flowing all around her, and moving inside her body. Her question lingers for our contemplation.

A Serpent Below

There was a cousin of Lympha named Melusine, a spirit of fresh water who belonged in a sacred spring. But once, for a brief time, Melusine passed as human. Until the day came when she had to leave, to live again in the wild as who she really was.

She appears in art as a woman who is a serpent or fish from the waist down. She sometimes has wings, tails, or both.

Melusine marries a nobleman under certain pledged conditions.

Such is the oath everlasting made by primordial Styx,
the river that gushes through treacherous caverns below.
(Theogony)

In their marriage vows, she required her husband to swear three oaths. First, to honor one day apart each week. Second, to respect her absolute privacy when she bathed. Third, he would never ask, or try to find out, what she was doing in her times of solitude. This made him curious.

The clue is here, in this very land:
discovery will clinch it.
What goes unobserved escapes.
(Oedipus the King)

Or so he reasoned.

Every sabbath day, Melusine would retire to her chamber, and from there, she slipped into caverns branching beneath the castle, not to be seen again until early light the next day.

She drew serene into the depths,
far beneath watered caverns,

84

beyond the touch of any human hand.

Alas, agreements between humans and water are fragile, even bolstered by threefold troths. One day her husband could no longer resist temptation. In one of the forbidden hours, he came to spy on her.

What spirit ever listened to a breaker of oaths?
(Medea)

He silently drew near. What was that sound of splashing inside her room? He crept forward, listening, and heard the most glorious singing; the song he once heard by the Roman ruins, near the fountain where they first met. Peering into her room through a crevice in the wooden door, he saw his wife in her bathtub, gazing out to the forest through the open window, crooning softly, smoothing her hair with a golden comb. She was like a vision out of Sappho.

Some say the most beautiful sight on the face of the earth
is a panoply of splendid horsemen drawn up for battle,
some say an army with windswept banners flying,
some say ships sweeping past a promontory in full sail,
but I say she, the one I love, is in any far vista singularly the
loveliest.
(Sappho)

But then he looked down. Down there.

Her exquisite limbs ended in a scaled and supple fishtail. She was splashing languid waves in gentle time as she trilled each opalescent note.

There is no home. That is over.
(Medea)

The prince cried out in terror, and Melusine's melody stopped. The window was propped open. Over the granite windowsill, she unfurled hidden wings, rose high above the fortress walls, and disappeared, never to return.

You handmaids, huddled protectively near her chamber —
does she who hid such dreadful power
still walk the halls, or has she abandoned this place?
Take my word: she will have to hide beneath the earth,
or rise to the uttermost air,
if she imagines she will escape unpunished from this household.
(Medea)

Broken pledges, winged evasions, and returns to her secret cavern frame legends of Melusine. Once she made her Medea-like escape, whether she was a mermaid, a dragon, or a serpent below was never certain. She could appear at noon as a heartbreakingly beautiful sprite, singing near a fountain deep in the forest, her face hidden by a green veil. At midnight she could rise from the cliffs beneath the stronghold as a snake with a golden key in her mouth, a key that would unlock any fortress. But she could not long fit into a human bath. Exposed as a goddess:

She flew beyond human vision, aloft between heaven and earth.
(Metamorphoses)

Once she flees from castle to cavern, from sabbath to season, from bath to her underground spring, she is no duplicitous creature. She is herself again. A companion to Lympha, a nymph of fresh water, she could not be any other.

Her husband's sorrow ran deep. He did not even notice his tears; how could he rinse them away? She had brought to him for her dowry the gifts of purification and salvation. Human sorrows, even princely or heroic ones, thirst for release through immersion. The hero Aeneas, who would one day father the Roman empire, could not be healed from the bloodshed of war until he was cleansed by a stream of living water. When Odysseus was drowning for all his transgressions in war, a goddess of the deep rose from the gulfs of the sea to lend him her lifesaving gossamer veil. He lived. At once:

> *she dove back into the billowing sea*
> *in the form of a long-winged seabird,*
> *and a dark wave closed to conceal her*
> *from his sight forever.*
> (Odyssey)

Heroes and husbands stand looking out over a sea or spring that seems empty. Melusine could not stay fixed in the palace, hidden behind keyholes in an artificer's bath. Her nature was bound to mystical caverns.

Though stories say Melusine bore children in the palace, no palace of shaped stone could be as generative as the place of her origin. Her birthplace was an otherworldly atmosphere suited to water spirits, where dripping swathes of moss, and tremulous footing were only slowly revealed. She moved playfully inside bright fountains in silent interiors, where the enigma of her lower body was secretive as a cave. Mythic caves birthed divinities and monsters, and Melusine partook of both.

His first glimpse of her was near the mouth of a cavern, an erotic place for an unequal meeting. Melusine was in her element. Dappled with green, moist as a lettuce garden, it was a place marked on no map, where cool verdant growth, and the sound of a gently trickling fountain offered no determined outcome but fertile possibilities: an irresistible sensual experience, an interlude of refreshing rest, the faraway ecstasy of private song and dance.

Such were the caverns where they first met. They say the nobleman had lost his way and wandered long from his path before he found her.

How to reverence such a being?

Will she look upon us face to face?
Will she listen to voices that try to name her?
(Medea)

If there could have been a different end to this story beyond what we know, it would flow from longing over long time. Imagine if Melusine's husband had become a nympholept. He might have grown in her absence, to see her again in rivulets that sometimes ran laughing along the forest trails, young companions who appeared and disappeared as they will. Trickles would become her ways of speaking; pebble beaches and hemlock roots would comb her hair. Glints and flashes of sun on water would be her mirth, the toss of her tresses, sparkle of glances, flash of pale ankle. Her course would change with every rain. Quicksilver, apart from slower beings of earth. Could he have loved, more than her captivity, such unexpected glances? Perhaps he did.

Today, in the place where her husband first saw her, across the broken bridge, they say an evergreen grows. Shading the ruins of the Roman fountain, they call it Melusine's tree. When you look, it is not always there.

The Girl

Like fawns sniffing spring newborn,
or lambs playfully frisking in soft meadows,
the maidens of Eleusis,
lifting the folds of their shimmering robes
to free their delicate arching feet,
dashed along the path to the sacred well
where they practiced circle dances,
their bright hair flowing
over their shoulders like breezes of crocus blossoms.
(Homeric Hymn to Demeter)

Let her be maiden, nymph, fawn, or lamb. Let her stand with the maidens of Homeric Eleusis whose hair is flowing on this page, arm in arm with a village's marriageable girls, or spring across a meadow with fetching maidens of romantic poetry and ancient vase painting. Let her be a blushing innocent or let her couple secretly with satyrs in a cave. A nymph has many epithets, wears them lightly, and is bound by none. Her coming looks like a dance because it is a dance. When art and myth were young, bands of nymphs entwined hands and stepped together in a circle. They are rich-tressed and deep-bosomed; they skip and twirl in fluid rhythm on graceful ankles. Free in her ballet, the nymph inspires longing as a barely discernible fragrance, the only trace of her passing. Her limbs are quick as morning glory stems, and coiled ringlets curl on her shoulders as she runs. Her hair and footsteps mirror the erotic form of *melam* energy, the arrows of desire that arced upward from Mesopotamian goddesses' shoulders.

She lives nearby but is rarely seen. She belongs to a chorus of mythic voices in the ancient Greek landscape, echoing across wild meadows. Echoing also from archives and excavations because she also lived in history. Mortal maidens danced in choruses for goddess festivals and played with dancing dolls.

Dolls were lovingly placed in girls' graves and in grottoes sacred to the nymphs. Some dolls had movable limbs, and had ensembles of shoes and headwear, even miniature vessels for the bridal bath. Young girls played with them, dressed them, wove fabric for them as they learned to weave, and dedicated dolls in sanctuaries of Artemis before the day of their wedding.

Girls and their mothers also carried a girl's own clothes to Artemis after betrothal, making votive offerings of the toys and textiles of her girlhood. When a girl on her gravestone holds her doll, this meant death came to her before she was wed. Her doll was called a nymph, just as the girl holding her would be.

In all her tender vigor, a young girl lived her springtime as a nymph, and archaic poetry rejoiced in her freedom to frisk. For the maiden, it was a brief season. Outside the circle of flower dances, she was a bride-to-be and mother-to-be, whose reproductive duty would determine the course of her life.

In Ancient Greek nymphē meant nubile girl, doll, wife until the birth of her first child (or first male child), or archetypal bride. It also meant a deity alive in her landscape, a goddess who invigorated cave, pool, spring, sea, tree, rock, grove, meadow, or mountain. As nympholepts knew, she inspired rapture in the wilderness. The word expresses the untamed energy that leaps up immortal in young girls.

When the wedding day dawned, bridal bath water was drawn from a pure spring a girl felt relationship with, or from nearby shrine-sheltered waters of a nymph. In some nymph shrines there were mystical cults for a girl's transition rites. Her rites of passage called to nymphs and to their chorus leader Artemis.

Transition was never without peril. Although she is virgin herself, Artemis keeps a watchful eye on menarche, marriage, and motherhood. Failure to complete a rite of passage made goddesses and heroines protective of mortals approaching that transition, because they knew its dangers better than anyone. Artemis was a fiercely, even savagely private, goddess. In myth, only her chorus of nymphs were permitted to enter her secret retreats and attend her lustrations. Historically, she held certain inner sanctums and shrines that forbade entrance to all but priestesses, and even then, with great caution, and only once a year. Religious prohibitions preserved her landscapes as untrodden and unentered. She was an "unbroken virgin," which meant untamed, undomesticated, and unmarried. As "a lion among women," she released mothers from childbirth pains into safe delivery or death. She made unsure footing for the safe passage of a bride, as her protection balanced on arrowpoint or cliff edge.

Her shrines were in the wilderness, on the rims of remote and unreliable frontiers.

The modesty of Artemis was inviolate. Once when the world was green, the legendary hunter Actaeon entered a sacred grove unbidden and dared to capture a glimpse of the goddess bathing in the recesses of a secret pool. It was more than a glimpse; catching the sound of nymphs at play, he crept forward to see better—a dangerous move. For trespassing on her nature preserve, into her sanctuary, and against her person, the mistress of wild animals turned the hunter into a stag, to be pursued for his pelt, his flesh, and the fine rack of antlers sprouting out of his head. Trespass and peering at what was forbidden were not his only offenses. Earlier he had hunted so furiously, as Ovid tells it, shouting heedlessly with his companions, that hillsides rang with his voice, and the forest floor ran with the blood of slain animals. Transformed as punishment into a stag himself, the hounds he had trained for the pursuit and killing of wild beasts went wild and tore him apart. As they attacked, as he grew fur and hooves, he tried and tried to speak, to call their names, to make them obey.

But they had cast off the yoke of names. So had he. And it is
not in the nature of the wild to obey.

A hyacinth sprang up in the crevice of a distant mountain.
We sat together for an afternoon, me keeping respectful distance.
He got only a few hours of light in that crevasse.
I hiked out again to visit the valiant stem next day.
On the ground the deep red blossom curls, trampled, seeping,
the one I knew for a single afternoon.
Boot tracks all around.
(Sappho)

There are groves that should never be entered. Entrance, even
well-intentioned, turns a trackless meadow into known territory.
Eventually, trespass leads to claiming. Sappho knew this.

Her blossom lyrics, torn and used to wrap the dead, were
discovered in an ancient Egyptian trash heap.

Yet the truth of wilderness, in the region sacred to Artemis,
is that all along the margins, in every cranny and crevice, spring
up weeds, unclassified and unmapped, slanting between erected
portal and trackless land. These weeds are like unverifiable stories.
Crones and holy hags might cackle together at the common
definition of a weed anyway: a plant not desired, a plant of no
use or beauty. Especially since the word *hag* originally meant *holy*.
Human-drawn borders shift on the face of the earth because they
are imaginary, like masks worn by the chorus of a Greek tragedy,
removed at the end of the play. Outside city limits, where maps
hesitate in lingering doubt, exists the living hyacinth. Somewhere
out there Artemis ranges, whole and vibrant. Also out there
somewhere strides Nemesis, her scales of justice in one hand and
her unsheathed sword in the other: the implacable goddess who
redresses wrongs against the natural order.

Artemis had many cult titles. For a young girl, worshipping

she of the turning point,
she who withers or ripens,
she who loosens the virgin's sash,
she who sets free from labor pangs,

might mean survival through her precarious reproductive journey. Dying in childbirth was the fate of many *nymphai*. Ever wild, the severe and merciful goddess who proclaimed her own virginity accepted virginal offerings, but as "shedder of arrows," her bow is near to hand, her aim unerring. As the mortal maiden steps from virgin meadow to birthing bed, skirting reproductive risk, somewhere on the border Artemis is watching.

Another goddess of maiden death was watching too: Persephone. She experienced withdrawal, devastation, and return with every cycle of seasons. As the goddess of budding springtime, from her birth, Persephone was called a sweet flower, delicate seedling, and tender branch.

As Demeter's daughter, Persephone rose in not one delicate seedling, but in every bud. Easily she formed a chorus, and protected girlhood friendships that lasted beyond death.

This dust is what is left of lovely Timas,
who perished before her friends could adorn her bridal chamber.
Instead, Persephone prepared a place for her
to comfort and welcome her to dark halls.
Afterward, the girls she held most dear
took sharp iron, cut their hair,
and sacrificed their silky tresses to garland her tomb.
(Attributed to Sappho)

Wilderness proliferated in ancient imagination to create goddesses and nymphs, and girls, ever elusive. Maidens of Eleusis, Persephone, Artemis, Inanna, and Timas, variable, seasonal, and dynamic, always coming into being and always passing away.

An archaic poet could never aspire to name them all; he could not have done it if he had a Homeric throat of iron and a tongue of bronze and could go on singing forever. No one could have done it for another reason too: only reverent life alongside them might gain their trust, to reveal their secret names.

We are a chorus of daughters,
sacrosanct, lovely, soft-glancing, beguiling, robed with dawn.
We are countless delicate-footed nymphs of lively step,
shining offspring of goddesses, who rove in throngs
to invigorate the living earth and teeming waters.

Learning our names would be too hard for any mortal.
But still...someone who lived prayerfully,
some keeper of oaths born near to us,
might in time come to learn one of our names.
(Theogony)

Nymphs evoked all that is shrouded in mist and lesser known. Only country mortals who lived lives bound to local earth could call on spirits of familiar streams, trees, and caves. Natives of a place, who were honored to call local nymphs by name, invoked them for human needs, and asked them to heal relationships between people and wild places.

Like blossom clusters, a nymph is rarely singular. But in a rare moment, while she herself was alone, the lyric poet Sappho looked up after apple harvesters had gone and saw a single blushing girl.

A sweet apple blushes on the high branch tip,
high on the highest twig, and goes unnoticed—
no, not unnoticed. They glimpsed her; she escaped.
Apple pickers were not able to reach her.
(Sappho)

Sappho invites us to see herself standing in the apple grove, as a poet who lives in gardens, glades, and sanctuaries haunted by nymphs. Listening to cold streams rush, watching the moon rise, delighting in blossoms, pitying a fallen hyacinth, feeling the same emotions as apples do. Even slants of light tremble and move in harmony in this orchard, the most perfect setting for the aching beauty of *lanthanein*. The sweet apple goes unnoticed, forgotten by all but Sappho, and in her poetry she blushes forever. Sometimes Sappho named her girls, silver stars around the shimmering moon, choruses of brides-to-be. Sometimes they are nameless. She was gifted to sing as her throng of maidens left her for marriage, one by longed-for one. But even alone, she makes us feel that oaks, streams, and moon-shadowed roses felt with her. And her musical instrument too.

Speak to me, divine lyre; be born for me in your voice.
(Sappho)

Syrinx was a nymph who was transformed into a musical instrument to be played by the wind. She sings on quiet riverbanks. As the youngest maiden of Eleusis in the chorus who first opened this section gravely says, "The gifts of the gods are gifts no mortal can refuse, nor have for the asking." She is Kallidikê unwed, whose name means The Goddess of Justice is Beautiful.

However far away her chorus, Sappho is still singing.

The Treasures of Darkness

One night in late antiquity, by flickering lamplight while the pagan world was fading, a trusted servant dug quietly. He was burying a hoard of silver treasures underneath the mosaic floor of a luxurious Roman villa. The earth would keep them safe on the Esquiline hill of Rome until the times of trouble had passed. These were the exquisite bridal gifts of his educated, wealthy mistress, and he gave them one last darkening look. Cupids, Muses, goddesses of fortune, serpent-centaur sea gods, and bare-breasted Venus in a seashell graced these vessels — along with a Christian inscription. Were they hidden away because it was it unwise to display such wealth when rabble threatened, or when troubled religions frowned? No one ever came back for them.

In the rubble of a dying civilization or in the grave, it was hoped the earth would hold all safe against her breast. Inside the Sumerian royal tombs of Ur, consorts, craftsmen, soldiers, and servants sat down in the tomb alive, holding poisoned clay cups. In the best-preserved and richest tombs, all the mortals within, since the day they were born, had been moving toward the treasures of darkness.

In the grave, richly adorned harpists were bidden to play forever and rise beyond decay. These female musicians died as sacrifices for their queen. When the death pit was found undisturbed, scores of women leaned in row against the walls, perhaps still holding their instruments, or perhaps they had been taken gently from their unfurling hands. One of the women had a harp laid on her skull.

The ritual had come, looked for since midwives had cut their navel-cords. Laid out shoulder to shoulder, elegantly gowned, draped in jewels. Styled in elaborate chignons interwoven with thin sheets of silver ribbon, wreathes, and diadems. Cloaks pinned in place with precious works of art. Musicians, singers, celebrants, comforters. Hair ribbons gleaming against dark soil in a trench showed excavators the women were there.

Make gentle welcome of the newly captive girl.
She was the chosen flower of many treasures,
and nothing is familiar to her here.
As she must stay and bear her yoke,
let her new masters bear compassion.
(Agamemnon)

In the afterlife, Mesopotamian harpists play their melodies at the feast. Radiant lyres and voices throb, hair ribbons and fragrant blossoms are bright as the days when singers sang their first melodies. In the earth above their feasting, a little girl curled in one royal death pit, holding a corroded coil of silver ribbon in her fist. She did not have time to arrange it in her hair. No one warned her:

They will offer you food of death. Taste it not.
They will offer you water of death. Touch it not.
(Nergal and Ereshkigal; Inanna's Descent)

Was she part of a glorious ritual, happy, beautifully dressed, and feasted? She may have been given to the palace to fulfill a parent's vow. If so, she may have known her fate all along. If she realized what was happening only that day, it may have been by unusual signs. Cooks preparing a smaller feast than would be needed to feed everyone after the ceremony; reed mats hiding the earthen walls; oxen facing out with the wrong grooms at their heads; guards in the entrance, facing in. But each of these signs could be interpreted another way. Different versions may have been whispered in the pit right up to the last moment.

She may have been solemn with responsibility: her own cup to drink from, textiles finer than she had ever worn before, and the silver ribbon for her hair. The poison may have taken hold too soon for her to finish dressing. Did she wonder what a palace in the underworld would look like? Was she proud or frightened that her life was a gift that belonged to her ruler?

In her Assyrian palace, a young queen's remains show that must have spent the latter portion of her young life trying to conceal her rotten teeth. They are laid bare now, though her tomb has been bulldozed by a modern regime. The diadem she was buried in, plaited of pure gold, still rests in a museum. No matter how much circlets shimmer, grave metals gleam darkly like the netherworld's golden bough. Dug up from the Great Below, icons and ram-headed harps are delivered as illustrious treasures to museums and retain the darkness where they emerged. Restored Roman mosaics lapsed into rubble again under museums of warring Europe. The golden "treasure of Helen" went mysteriously missing after excavation at Troy. No wonder Isaiah and Sumerian scholars called these things treasures of darkness. Shattered, looted, and reassembled vases have been lost and lost again: all these objects speak their knowledge of withdrawal, devastation, and return. Then they slip into the ground to be unearthed once more—over and over.

Time in long innumerable years brings forth all unseen,
reveals them for a moment, then envelops them again.
(Ajax)

Such riches are redolent with the unguents of subterranean temples. When prized treasures, horses, oxen, and humans were buried, they were called sacred. Needed in the next world, the living laid down, then rose again to perpetual service. They were called beloved when consigned to death. We might call them palace or temple personnel. To accompany the funeral rites of Gilgamesh, to staff his netherworld palace, we saw that an immense beloved retinue laid down beneath the river.

In images of the psalmist, their hearts poured out, their bones scattered, and they were given to dust.

Scribes recorded the goods to be delivered to palaces underground. They used the new technologies of writing. Then in their turn, the ledgers and the scribes who had written them proceeded to the Great Below.

Praise be to Nisaba, goddess of writing.
(cuneiform tablet formula)

What were leaders like who kept such records and accepted such sacrifice? Did they believe that their stomachs should always be full?

To maintain his supremacy:

Kronos, king of primal gods, kept gobbling down his children,
then Earth made sure to craft a trick herself.
He seized a huge stone and crammed it in his stomach,
before he could stop himself.
She had made him think it was his youngest child,
not a stone in swaddling clothes.
She knew he was hard-hearted.
(Theogony)

Where did appetite end? Palaces boasted decorative panels extolling Assyrian royal hunts, depicting lions and lionesses in death throes, pierced with weapons, gushing blood from open mouths. We do not have far to go to reach the blood sport of wild animal massacres in the Roman arena that caused the decline and extinction of sought-after species. They may have been easy habits to fall into, these amusements of feasting and laceration. In whatever way the habits evolved, at some point humans came to believe that all we wanted to be ours should be ours.

Angered by willful blindness, gods grind to dust human plans.
(Medea)

Because the land and city were his, a king could divert waters
and irrigate it. Because it was his, he could set others to work
with grove-felling axe. They labored for his vision.

The Prince established safe dwellings,
divided spacious sheepfolds, and
served out cropland in portions.
He distributed tools, and set up a standard
to distinguish between city, field, and farm.
(Enki and the World Order)

This is Enki hard at work again, ordering the world and mapping
it out. The oldest known map in the world comes from the region
of the sacred city of Nippur.[7] It does not simply depict land
but identifies canal-bordered areas as economic allotments. The
grain grown on each field is labeled, destined for elite tables.
Places bore names like these:

palace field, temple field, pasture for the diviner priest, orchard for
the retired soldier.
(Nippur Map Tablet)

How much was left for the growers?

Land was conceived as a patchwork of units, divided into
paternal estates. Fields began to be named for administrative
and legal purposes. Archives of clay tablets grew, piled with
private deeds of ownership that described real estate and its
value in detail. This is a clue about why maps came into being
and why the new idea caught on.

Maps, writing, naming, and counting organized mountains
of goods and channeled rivers of wealth. On monuments, kings

and queens began to say, "I did this." When Oedipus was cast forth on the mountainside to die, the king did this "by the hands of others." Other hands belonged to regal hands, and lowly others did not attempt to name themselves for eternity.

Some old field maps still hinted at stories:

field of doves,
huluppu meadow,
sheepfold scoured by wind.
(Nippur Map Tablet)

Now, old maps and palace records, scribal hand-bones, and royal stomachs are tumbled with laborers' pickaxes and long consumed by earth. Buried lists of goods are word-hoards that flared briefly against oblivion. On the banks of a river, or under palace walls, whether they were wrapped for safekeeping or not, they have all found earth's equality in being dug, scythed, winnowed, and digested.

The king in his palace lies on his deathbed,
his shrines are locked and barren with dust.
He has fallen like cypress, boxwood, or cedar,
no palace pleasures ease his pain.
Never again will he rise to his feet.
(The Death of Gilgamesh; The Death of Ur-Nammu)

It was customary to close treasures over with a protective curse engraved in stone:

If anyone disturbs this cache,
removes my grave goods,
defaces my image,
alters my inscriptions —

Never mind. We learned to dig right past such measures.

In stolen moments, did the unfree ever wander outside the estate, temple, or palace? Did grain-growers take long walks across the fields of priests and palace officials? Did they sometimes bury what meager treasures they had, or illicit tablets, work of a hired scribe? For what purpose? Just to preserve or say something, anything, that escaped their ruler's notice? Did they know that

the Red-headed woodpecker lives in marshes of snags and hides its cache of food in splintered wood. It stores grasshoppers alive, wedged so tightly into a crevice that they cannot escape.

But the bird stores just what he needs to eat. Nothing more.

A larder, a treasure trove. The grasshopper waits. The worker wedged in his crevice digs. The grasshopper sings. I write. We speak. I keep uncovering treasures of darkness, the sour and sweet inextricable, the price of inexpressible beauty being inexplicable sorrow. Maybe only those who know the one can hear the other.

Skylla

First footprints on trackless meadow. A nymph is sighted.

Odysseus decided to sail a course than ran dangerously close to the cave of a monster. He had to; it was the only open route to and from the underworld. But before he takes that dare in the *Odyssey*, the enchantress Circe gives him a warning: the monster Skylla has a tangled dog pack for a groin. Even in the world of myth this is surprising. Skylla is multiple beneath the waist, like a split seed exposed to light or an excavated forced bulb. Her horrid amalgamation disrupts categories and defies understanding. So does her voice.

In Ancient Greek laskein means a sharp and piercing sound. A visceral sound of instinct and emotion apart from any meaning. The word emits the ring of bronze on stone, the scream of a raptor on its prey, and the cry a she-monster makes just before she strikes. It also means shrieks and bones breaking with a crack. Of bitches, it means a gut-wrenching howl.

Skylla became a monster after pursuit by a god. She has this in common with snake-haired Medusa. Fiendish females are one effective way for nightmares to get our attention. If you have ever watched a shrew devour a worm, you know what it is to be horror-stricken, unable to watch, unable to look away.

But wait. In early days, Skylla was a nymph. Then through no fault of Skylla's, the transformatrix Circe, reduced to fighting for scraps of male attention, scattered noxious herbs into a pool to make her unsuspecting rival hideous. That way:

No one, not even a god, would have the courage to look at her.
(Metamorphoses)

When Skylla began to bathe, her loins erupted into a mass of wild female dogs emerging from her womb, permanently embedded upon her thighs. At first, she tried to escape them, then she realized she could not; they had become a part of her, and she could not shake them loose. She had become a bitch. She had become a whole den of them.

The god Skylla was disfigured for Glaucus. He first saw her unclad after she went swimming in a secluded cove. A virgin wary of males, the nymph avoided him. Glaucus was young and naïve himself, so he tried to lure her to his arms with compliments—not to her, but to a virgin meadow.

If you could only see it. A soft field of green by the coast, never grazed by gentle animals at all; not even bees have tasted its flowering nectar. This is a meadow no one has woven a garland from, and no scythe has ever touched. I was the first person who ever entered there.
(Metamorphoses)

Glaucus imagines that honeybees and herbivores would be too rough for this field. He likens maiden to meadow and hints that he has been her "first one." In his reverie, he abstains from garlands and disdains the scythe. He wants to reassure her, and himself, that he can enter the purity of a pristine field without impact, pluck a single blossom, and find possession sweet. Sweet unmixed with bitterness.

Stories about sensitive, doomed lovers are irresistible. Once these two have met, and courtship enters their idyll, tragedy seeps into the story.

After Glaucus woos her, and fatally reveals her favorite bathing haunt to Circe, Skylla's life as a nymph is over and existence as a monster begins. Her limbs branch out nether-wise in rage and appetite, exuberantly hideous. Formerly wandering

waves and shores, playing with her sister nymphs, she now
holes up alone in a cavern full of death. Formerly lithe, she now
crams snatched sailors into her gullet, as many as she can snatch
at once. Glaucus was a fishing god; now Skylla fishes for men
and eats them as they cry for help. Odysseus tells his audience
that her savagery of his companions was the most pitiful sight
he saw on all his wanderings: the sea-girl who was turned into
a ravenous hole by the desire to control and possess her.

A terracotta queen of night stands nameless,
molded of baked clay, the substance of creation.
Vivid once with ochre, no trace of paint remains.
Her quadruple horned helmet is for a goddess,
crowned by the disc of an inscrutable full moon.
Does she offer herself to menace or to charm?

She is fierce enough to appear wearing only a necklace,
bracelet, and a coiled length of rope in each upraised hand.
Does this mean she has conquered three of seven gates?

That archaic smile of private knowing,
flanked by owls who stare without expression —
owls or daughters or priestesses in flat masks.
Her folded wings match their feathered mantles.
She stands poised on the muscles of twin lions
who look out holding our gaze, about to spring into action.
Their eyes assess any who approach her.
Incisions on the clay beneath their feet
mean foothills, rocky places, desolation.

Her muscled calves sprout dewclaws,
her taloned toes grip. If she takes flight,
both owls will flank her. If she forsakes this plaque,
and shakes off all artistic restraint,

the lions will prowl around her,
and safeguard her desertion of this museum.
(Mesopotamian Queen of the Night plaque)

Like any wild creature, once she was seen, Skylla the nymph faced the danger of extinction. As a hybrid monster, Skylla could at least defend herself.

But unplanned hybrids were not only unnerving; they were disadvantageous. The control of breeding that drove early domestication projects was designed to weed out undesirable mixtures and make creatures and plants predictable. Babylonian priests recalled an era when humans could be born with horse, goat, or bird parts; when dogs, fish, or horses sometimes bore each other's heads or human faces. That story made humans shudder. Domesticators were not enthusiastic about category disruption, except in the outlet of myth. They liked things to be just so.

The iron tool wears a brilliant crown.
He digs canals, cleans ditches, opens furrows.
He helps build houses, compliant houses who hear the king.
Disloyal ones the tool tears down.
Kindly plants that are wholesome, he assists by loosening their
soil.
Malicious weeds, he tears off their heads.
(The Song of the Hoe; The Rulers of Lagash)

The domesticated were meant to emerge at birth with one carefully planned identity. Arts of animal husbandry were celebrated as semi-divine powers. But rigid control inevitably breeds monsters. Skylla never meant to stray from her original form; she was misled. Like her complex body, versions of her proliferated in ancient story. But all agree that she was once a lovely nymph.

When Odysseus told his captivated audience about his narrow escape from Skylla, he added one last touch to her portrait. It is not a plausible detail. Circe had foretold that Skylla's howling would be terror itself. And once he got near her lair, Odysseus did hear horrible shrieks. His ship was so far below the monster's cliffside cave that his men looked tiny, dangling above, once she hauled them out of the boat. Yet mixed with the cries of men and bones, Odysseus heard something softer. He says he heard a voice as faint as the mewl of a newborn puppy, a voice that sounded vulnerable.

Sailing past Skylla is not about realism. How could he have heard her so faint in the distance? Of all her strange and hybrid ruinations, this soft cry is most poignant.

Separated from her chorus, a nymph is endangered, like a tree alone, more vulnerable to tearing forces.

Somehow, from within the heart of the monster, we hear the maiden's voice.

Tropism

Look: beside streams in storms of winter,
trees yield to the wind to preserve their branches,
while those that stiffly oppose the wind perish root and branch.

In this image from Sophocles' tragedy *Antigone*, one man engages another using a metaphor drawn from the lifesaving bending of trees. It is Haemon, whose name means blood, counseling his father Creon, whose name means masterful ruler. Underneath his reasoning is a heartfelt plea:

Yield, I ask you. Please. Be willing in your heart to change.
No one wise holds ideas too rigidly.

Since this play is a tragedy, his father doesn't listen. Haemon's father is a newly installed king. He is in fact afraid to hear, to bend, to turn with the tempest rather than battle against it. To him those motions sound too close to submission—to Inanna bowing down. In fact, he defines himself by his organized and methodical control of untamed nature and willful women. Later in the play he says:

I swear that I am not a man, and she is the man instead,
if she can win this battle of wills with me.
(Antigone)

He goes so far as to condemn to death Antigone, Haemon's betrothed bride.

Who or what bends? Who or what doesn't? As a result, who or what survives? These questions might sound human, or they might sound vegetal. They recall where we began, where trees twisted to meet extreme conditions with grace. Here we enter the realm of plant ethics.[8]

As Haemon observed, even the most imposing tree is flexible from feeder-root to twig-tip. It is in constant motion where it stands. A tree's ability to flex and turn in response to an external stimulus is commonly called tropism. Tropism is a crucial survival move. For a plant, being pliant means being alive. This makes sense even at the cellular level; the cell membrane that doesn't pulse is dead.

Haemon's father, however, does not have bending or pulsing at the top of his list of survival or success strategies. No gatekeeper practiced those virtues. Would he then admire feebleness, weakness, or passivity?

When Aristotle chose a word for physical matter, he chose a word that generally meant wood. He was taking a complex stance, since he believed that plants had souls, an original guiding force inside: an *arkhē*. He considered this soul, however, weaker than the principle in animals. Is it weaker? If we were talking about humans, and not about rigid wintertime trees or ensouled plants, then weakness (bending in the wind) might be seen as effective passive resistance, and inscrutability (just being a plant, nothing to see here) might be a subtle or even undetectable way of escaping overbearing ideas. When Enkidu cursed the "senseless" cedar gate, it had no need to answer him.

If we side with Haemon and look to plants for ideas about how to live, we see that they bend to live cooperatively in community, and spontaneously and reciprocally share resource with others. This giving and yielding are what Haemon meant: a flexible tree gives way to the wind. Haemon was recommending that his father learn from a plant's mode of radical adaptation to the environment: what Thoreau saw in wild apple trees. On rocky slopes, bristlecone pines shrug and make do with what is. They are not known for being demanding or egotistic.

Even within their bodies, the ethos of plants does not form hierarchies. Roots in the soil and leaves in the sun, all parts of plants dance in flexible stability or stable flexibility. They do not deal in focal points. When plants perceive and feel, they sway and respond in every cell. Metaphors that flow right past central bureaucracy and civic concentration of power cannot help but spring to mind. In our own bodies, are we not organized around a spine and the central nervous system it protects? That seems like a tree trunk-like structure, but a gash to our trunk incapacitates us, while a tree is designed to stream around the wound.

Without a central pumping organ, a sycamore lifts water many stories high into the air. The tree lifts nutrients to share the soil's food with her leaves. This is how lymph—not blood—slowly moves in our bodies. The beech has no need for a specialized heart or brain because she is designed in flowing layers throughout. There is no heart or brain in one spot that could stop the whole tree.

If we became more like trees, would we become more giving and peaceful? Sounds idyllic. But wait. If giving and sharing do not seem too passive for comfort, how plantlike do we need to become? Are we willing to take root? If we are, doesn't immobility seem somehow paralyzing? Will we end up in what is called a vegetative state?

The rootedness of plant ethics might inspire dread. Humankind prefers escapes. But since a plant does not abandon its place, it must live with what happens to its environs. No matter what. Like Haemon's father, many humans would shun such deep dependence. But plants stake their lives on solving local and communal issues. They cannot, do not, run away. They might show us how to do the same. Where they are rooted, trees comprehend sky, kin, soil, stream, and underworld. They know the earth better than we do. From the perspective of ancient mythology, that breadth of comprehension sounds strikingly divine. Divine awareness makes sacred ground of any place a plant takes root.

Surely the capacity for profound, intimate relationship is a gift. For rootedness, some ancients took vows that were treelike. A much-transplanted tree doesn't thrive. Commitment to a Pythagorean community or a monastic order meant that initiates stayed put. Their oaths were vows of stability.

The fungus-backed oak who has fallen onto the forest floor to decompose has taken such a vow and keeps it.

Aphrodite described how the lives and deaths of nymphs and trees were bound together in a beloved place.

The nymphs of this mountain are not like mortals or immortals.
They mingle with lovers in the secret desire of caves.
The hour the nymphs are born, in that very same hour
fir trees and lofty oaks are born; they flourish together
on abundant Earth's breast and holy mountain peaks.
They stand magnificent, arms lifted to the sun.
They themselves are known as sanctuaries of the gods.
Mortals do not go near them with iron.
When at last the day of death draws near,
first the wondrous trees grow dry in the soil,
the bark that cloaks them withers, and limbs fall.
Then the single soul shared by tree and nymph departs,
and leaves behind the light of the sun.
(Homeric Hymn to Aphrodite)

A nymph did not somehow live *inside* her tree; in a personified form she was the life of the tree. From Aphrodite's words, we might revision Lilith's house as the soul of the tree, departing the huluppu when death came.

An elder beech falls to make room for sunlight to enter the canopy. Rotting meat is Inanna's chrysalis for return. As Epicurus taught, the elements inside our bodies are needed by future life. We turn into it even if we refuse to turn toward it. Whatever else might happen, we become the material that made us.

Opposition to nature, the well-worn nature vs culture dialectic of the belted hero, seems to have become a habit. But what if we didn't define ourselves by that subject-object stance? By the Sumerian bull-wrestling image of constant battle? To meet with trees who were his friends through the course of many years, Thoreau trekked miles through deep snowdrifts. He understood plants as equals or betters and might have appreciated a tree-truth that could be appended to Haemon's speech: willingness to befriend a plant relaxes our grip on all that lives.

How do we unlearn dichotomies: civilized and uncivilized; domesticated and wild; feeble vs. strong, control vs chaos? Don't we define ourselves by contrasts—partly by not being plants? By identifying all kinds of things that we are not, whether wild beasts, gods, demons, outsiders, or monsters? The otherness of plants might not be admired by all. Enki tore up and devoured the eight seedlings.

The truth is that lacking faces or opposable thumbs, plants are all but invisible to most human eyes. Socrates himself said, "Trees have nothing to teach me," though with characteristic irony he prefaced and followed that statement with detailed appreciation of his tree-shaded surroundings, especially the lovely plane trees and chaste trees beside a shrine and sacred spring. He even suggested that he was in danger of being possessed by the nymphs of the place. His dialogue *Phaedrus* beside the Ilisos River is all about longing and wonder—not certainty. Without the nymph-haunted afternoon beside the river to set the scene, without trees to shade the shrine, his philosophical questions would stand bare words in glaring sunlight. The intrigue of interlaced branches draws the listener in.

What about the fungi growing beneath the philosopher's feet? What might we learn or unlearn from mycelium, the interwoven fungi that form a vast sentient underground web upon which life—all of life—depends? Unlike animals, but like plants, fungi do not predetermine a certain number of shoots, limbs, or threads, but grow them in response to changing conditions. Prehistoric ancestors of trees shed not only their leaves, but their root systems in annual rhythms. This is change in repose; it is perennial withdrawal, exploration, and return. Alert to gods of the Great Below, underworld myths explored minds that responded with astute awareness to life on the surface. Were these gods born of fungus filaments? Or the personified consciousness of roots?

We can go further. Ironically, because the plant does not generally choose to speak—except through myth—a plant never lies. It is wise to qualify bald statements, however, simply noting that plants do not seem to speak audibly to most people. We evolved to journey together with companions of moss and willow, and the spirituality of plants for shamans and healers stretches deep into our shared *arkhē*.

Haemon's advice to his father keeps getting better and better. Are we not aware that mortals are rash? That speed is inherently stressful? That well-considered decisions require time for gathering emerging evidence, intuitions, emotions, counsel, and ideas? Human urgency to get somewhere, anywhere, is recklessly devouring the earth. It is Haemon's tragedy that his father acts swiftly and independently, and scorns patient deliberation with anyone. Nemesis is watching the plot. Like a strike of environmental retribution, a *katastrophê*, her revenge comes swiftly, before the play is over, in a single day.

Yet Emerson rightly perceived most justice as slow and organic, like mature fruit that coils waiting inside a dormant seed.

Plants are not swift. Their ethos spreads over a long time compared to ours. Under ordinary conditions, tropism is too slow for us to see. Left alone, many plants outlive us, and know their landscape profoundly. Staying in one place is something ancient people did more commonly than humans do today; they experienced throughout their lifetime the subtle changes in native ecologies around them. One thing Eros loves is slow and gradual fullness of coming-to-know. How different is the modern love of speed. When we travel too much, too fast, between landscapes, it must be harder to hold any of them as sacred, or to let them hold us as we whiz by.

But the "art of speeding" was one of the *mes*.

So perhaps we should patiently deliberate.

A long time ago, so long ago that we may as well say once upon a time, we parted hands and began our resolute journey away from trees. We developed the ability to move around and began our nomadic journey to leave them behind. Plants did not follow. Instead, they developed the ability to send roots into the soil. It was so long ago that many people forgot how to understand plant dialects, or our ancestral life in common with them. And they will not remind us, for as we learned to talk, they grew more silent, reserving their speech. Their hidden harmony is stronger than the one we are used to hearing. The obvious harmony is the sound of our own voices. The hidden harmony sheds words like wind, inside the sacred landscape. Now, surrounded by earth's plentiful raiment of plants, it is as if we somehow feel we stand alone, longing for the murmur of green voices slanting away just beyond the range of ordinary hearing.

Once I knew this perfectly. But I had forgotten.
(Oedipus the King)

In turning away to defend ourselves staunchly, and in viewing ourselves as organisms who are more than plants, higher life forms over lower ones, we lost our sense of kinship, and isolation spread like a contagion to every other organism we encountered. This vanished choice to turn away, to part hands, that we almost remember making, is expulsion from the primordial garden, self-imposed.

Sumerian myth remembers another creation.

In distant years when fates took root, the land was greening. Then one springtime, humans began to appear, pushing up like shoots, unfurling their heads from the soil.
(Enki's Journey to Nibru)

Tropism is a turning toward life, as samaras turn to position themselves in the earth.

Shall we turn toward plants?

To sum up Haemon's advice, while humans experimented with escapism, trees perfected stability. While we refined above-ground vision, hierarchy, feuds, chatter, and speed, plant choices were radically different. They chose silence, flexibility, and attunement balanced above and below the ground, with changes made slowly and cooperatively. In the sacred landscape, we chose mobility, they chose fidelity.

To borrow an environmental dialect, a trophic cascade is a tropism too, moving in either direction. As we restore respect for plants back into narratives that have largely excluded them, we look to heal the violence of humanity against our wisest kin.

Shall we turn toward plants?

Their mode of living might be described as abundant life, grounded above and below, in mutually caring relationship. Surely this is one description of flourishing in a sacred landscape.

Birch and cherry, beech and maple, nymph and fir entwine their roots to live and die together. Ancients envisaged this union for a mythical mortal couple, Baucis and Philemon, a husband and wife who were compassionate to impoverished strangers and cherished a temple and its sacred landscape throughout their long lives. As aged caretakers after long and devoted service to the sanctuary, one day they metamorphosed into mutually loving trees. This was in accordance with their wish.

Elders who were born here know this sacred place. They point out the two trees that grew together into one. I myself have seen prayer

garlands interwoven with their branches, and I have hung up fresh wreaths there as a suppliant. Side by side, the couple shade the portals of the temple, in twin trunks that unite two bodies: oak and linden in loving embrace.
(Metamorphoses)

As forest ecologists and botanists realize, plants share resources, graciously make way for each other, and communicate beyond our ken. In other words, they show love.

Surrounded by prolific life, how can we say:

In my grief I have come outside to be alone.
Only earth and air will hear my sorrows.
(Medea)

Others will hear. We are never biologically alone, no more than Archedamos was alone in his cave. As organisms we are not even one, or a unitary solitude ourselves, given that we are complex walking biomes. But even outside our bodies, we always stand in some real and sacred landscape, inside the awareness of plants. And all other sentient beings. The mycelium feels our footprint, every step.

Plant ethos is far older than Aristotle's plants with souls. Plant communities and plant spiritualities have always held us. Plant ethics have budded and are growing beyond mythic metaphor.

If we long for revelations, they are all around us. If we turn toward them, very slowly.

Terrible is the Beauty of Her Face

Originally a prehistoric nature divinity who brought buds and girls to blossom, once the written word begins, her epithets leap from goddess to whore. From archaic times, Spartans worshipped her as a heroine. Before and after death, when she appeared, she did not simply appear; she made epiphanies.

This is Helen of Troy, notorious for one journey, though she was famously born from a swan's egg as a daughter of Zeus and walked in her own right as princess and queen. Her lovely-haired chorus of companions gathered crocuses and trailed bright ribbons in song and dance, calling back and forth along the banks of her childhood river Eurotas. Versions of her seductions, disguises, and escapes trailed through Sparta, Egypt, Anatolia, and then further still. Now her sanctuaries sleep under rock-strewn slopes and pomegranate groves.

Kyras Vrysi, Cold Spring, forgotten even by shepherds, between the temple of Poseidon, the Roman bath, and the sleeping shrine of a child hero. A single afternoon behind the excavation house, light filtering through the lemon grove, dappled water deep between moss boulders in a cleft beyond the hills. Cool refuge from bright sun. The scented air dappled with jasmine, veiled with dusky thyme, swathed with gnarled aromas of silvered rosemary. Cold fruit and a paring knife, the day's bread, trickles of the spring drifting away into afternoon sleep. Dusty feet and chill water, licking honey from hands. A blanket beneath the olive trees felt against the skin forever. If Helen is anywhere, she still walks here.

The most fragrant secret of the most beautiful woman who ever lived is that her beauty was balm for other women. As a heroine, if parents evoked her name, she could miraculously appear, touch an infant girl, and make her marriageable. Sacrifices to her in her heroine cult could bring a woman the gifts of *hili*.

Helen herself became a much-married heroine. She brought unexpected dowries, including immortality by association. Her first husband learns that he will not die but will enter the blessed Elysian Field "because Helen was your bride and made you son-in-law to Zeus." If Helen had been aligned with gatekeepers, she might have led a stable life as a famed beauty, a prized possession of one man. As it is, she pays for being a substantiation or avatar of Inanna and Aphrodite, poised and energetic adversaries of any status quo.

Helen never made sense to men but escaped them every time. She had to, on evenings when her husband and his friends began to dwell on her biography again. And when escape was inconvenient, she had the verbal skill to tell persuasive stories, and pharmaceutical knowledge to shield herself from reprisals. She mixed soothing combinations of oratory and herbs.

She slipped a medicine into the wine bowl
where they were dipping their cups:
cure for heartache, remedy for bitterness,
to cast all sorrow and regret into oblivion.
This was one of the artful herbs Helen had come by
on her Egyptian travels, the gift of a foreign hostess.
(Odyssey)

Dexterity was useful for a wife brought back by force to Sparta from erotic adventures in Troy. And throughout her later life too. She is the face the oak finds beautiful all the days of women's fresh, wrinkled bark-body lives. Such wanton admiration of true loveliness, such adoration for women's lifelong charm, such unpredictably greening pleasure, gleams unexpected in Bronze Age poetry. As evocation of sacred epiphany, such attraction is alien to conventional beauty in its domesticated forms.

Walk alone in the blossoming wild, and Helen may appear as the face or the sapling that launched a thousand mysteries.

Cloaked as olive, veiled as hawthorn, robed as hemlock, yet recognizable.

The eternal *nymphē*, poised on the cusp of marriage.

Long before the exotic intrigue of Paris, her first abduction took place locally, in the meadows of home, but did not get far, when she was a flower-bud-faced girl. A *nymphē* playfully dancing riverside with her chorus, she was abducted by the aged king Theseus. They say he was smitten at first sight. Like a Sumerian god he had lurked beside the waters, around the threshing floors, dancing grounds, and vineyards of the river Eurotas. Her brothers, twin heroes, leapt into pursuit and brought her back home to Sparta. Found broken in a nearby sanctuary to Artemis, votive clay offerings of young girls dancing may remember that day.

In time and tongue among the jasmine-twined olive groves, in honor of her powers of regeneration (or in acknowledgment that she never bore a son), those closest to Helen still call her "nymph" and "bride" twenty years after she has arrived in Troy. We recognize the elusive wildness in that betrothed word: the remoteness and fierceness of a deity hidden in a sacred place. Both definitions attempt to capture the bridal Helen in procession, carrying the richest of dowries abroad, holding destiny even in her given name: *Helen*, which meant captive.

Who is it who named you so flawlessly?

Helen, bride of spears, draped in battles,
ship-destroyer, man-destroyer, fortress-destroyer,
lightly glimpsing out from under delicate and costly veils.

Her delicate glance is an arrow shaft,
a blossom of desire that devastates the heart.
(Agamemnon)

Longing runs millennia deep to catch a glimpse of this fatal blossom, this ambiguous bride. Witnesses on the ramparts shudder:

Terrible is the beauty of her face, her likeness to an immortal goddess.
(Iliad)

Myths of Helen may have had their genesis in many eyewitnesses. In Bronze Age elite women's lives, in traditions of abduction-marriage, in Aphrodite-worship, or in fears of the disorderly feminine. As the archetype of the destruction that an independent female agent could bring to patriarchal society, her face that launched a thousand ships has inspired countless reflections. Her far-flung travels, supernatural glamour, semi-divine birth, command of medicines, tantalizing charm, and unique afterlife inspired ancient writers to create a complex mythology of her adventures and misadventures. Was this "five-husbanded" heroine, who composed her own alternative version of the Trojan War, perfectly chaste as one philosopher called her? Did she never actually go to Troy, as several poets claimed? Was she some bloody portent or double agent? Blameless war victim or insightful prophet?

According to some versions, Helen was not only Aphrodite's double, but was a woman with her own living image. Only that lifelike phantom was fought for on the Trojan plain. We know that portrait statues of Helen were full of animation, lifelike, and compelling. Whether she showed the face of untouchable Artemis or sensuous Aphrodite, Helen should not be affronted in any form.

When he was blinded because his poetry criticized Helen, the archaic poet Steisichorus composed a poem to apologize to her, claiming he had been mistaken:

You never went near the benched ships,
you have never been to Troy.
(Palinode)

That instant, she restored his vision.

Allure embodied, she is not fixed, not in place, time, or identity. She is the preternaturally, or even eerily, beautiful double of the goddess of sexual impulse, Aphrodite. The word "identity" comes from Latin meaning "again and again." Not for her the again-and-again footpath between women's chambers, oven, birthing hut, and well.

A prostitute was pictured as a woman who traveled, a woman seen in the street, who put her foot outside her door to cross the paths of men. This could also describe a sorceress. Even a girl who looked out a window could be suspected of being:

a virgin above and an experienced woman below.
(Praxilla)

But Helen will not be secluded indoors; she will not stay put; she will not even stay mortal.

This is one reason why goddesses and heroines have so many faces, names, and epithets. Feminine allure could be a monstrous, metamorphosing hazard. A woman who was too mobile might turn out to be snake-tailed or winged with talons. The captivating horror of glamor echoes in our word "gorgeous," linguistic descendent of the Gorgon. This makes the Helen who ravishes viewers akin to category defying Skylla, Lilith, and Hekate of the crossroads. Artemis of wilderness was also identified with wandering Helen. A woman who died might be asked in the underworld whether she had encountered the roving huntress:

Did Artemis the archer find you and destroy you with her arrows?
(Odyssey)

But relocation might not be death; it might mean marriage.

Marriage brought risks; the virgin and her underworld bridegroom made an ancient widespread theme. For Helen, liaisons come and go. Never mind that the boundary being crossed is her own body. But some fierce spirit does mind. Remember Inanna:

She polishes her weapon — then ties dainty sandals on her feet.

Which Helen, heroine, or nymph faces us on any battlement, depends on the dynamism of the moment. Like nettle, in seasons young and tender or stinging and bold, her stinging might even be good to stimulate. Depending. As with herbal medicines, like those Helen commanded, so with nymphs. Where properties are fluid, presentation is too. Any encounter with liminal bride, water nymph or landscape deity is uncanny. How we approach, what we offer, expectations we bring, and who we are willing to become — all are noted and responded to. This is the reason why stories about nymphs, sprites, spirits vary so widely. We have already encountered figurines of Aphrodite with faces of so-called repulsiveness; perhaps some of Helen's epiphanies were also meant to repel. Perhaps her gorgeous Gorgonish allure could turn beholders to stone.

Allure embraces opposites. In keeping with this mythic theme, some tales of Helen did contain slander. Storytellers wondered what happened to abducted queens on rowing benches among the sailors, and in the beds of ardent captors. She asks herself, "Was I born a monstrous portent for all men?" In Troy, Helen proclaimed herself shameless: a bitch or whore. She is the only woman to accuse herself so in all archaic Greek poetry. Perhaps slyly. If she self-identifies low, no one else need attack with a slur. Ask a female stray: run-to-ground can be a sharp strategic vantage point for gnawing further plans.

She has no home but a ruin,
seeks shelter by the city wall.
When she sneaks a drink of water,
it is only enough to moisten her lip.
When she snatches a crumb to eat,
they drive her away with blows:
"No one you know is dining here!"
A curb at the crossroads is her bed,
hearing the hawkers quarrel,
watching the feet of passers-by.
(Iliad; Epic of Gilgamesh)

Sheltered inside the women's quarters, inside fortification walls, Helen weaves. It is an admirably domestic setting and activity for a woman. But she sits a world away from home, weaving a scarlet tapestry that portrays her own version of the war she watched from the battlements, the war being fought "for her."

She was weaving on her great loom
a prodigious textile of deepening folds,
an embroidered robe of rarest red,
stitching into it the countless battles
between Trojan tamers of horses
and Achaeans armored in bronze.
Battles they endured for her sake—
that is what they said, for her sake—
under the hand of the god who loves the carnage of war.
(Iliad)

No one has ever seen this textile. These few lines describing her working at her loom are our only clue. All we can say is that this web portrayed the struggles of the Trojan war. It was the conflict seen from Helen's own authoritative point of view. In an inner chamber, Helen as the very image of the goddess of love, weaves a robe, a perfect offering for a goddess.

Handwoven textiles were expressive artworks, even beyond death for tragic heroines.

On your grave, Iphigeneia,
women will sacrifice for you
meticulous weaving,
patterns unfinished,
left behind on silent looms:
textiles found in the women's chambers
after their weavers have died in childbirth.
(Iphigeneia among the Taurians)

Silent looms, abandoned for the final contest of childbirth, seem to stand in place of speech. Was Helen's artwork exoneration, protest, a correction of Homer's epic? Was her version in linen bordered with blooms she remembered from the banks of the Eurotas?

The elders on the ramparts of Troy, too old to fight but young enough to notice Helen, look at each other and say, "Lovely as she is, let her leave this city." She is desired everywhere and welcome nowhere.

Too many comings and goings. A woman did not quest; she settled down at home.

In the end, her roots burst walls, and the blossom that fractured hearts with longing shattered the bonds of naming and the bonds of fixing. Who was Helen? No definition, king, poem, or history captured her. The world's most famous Bronze Age captive, most renowned transplanted *nymphē*— worshipped, feared, reviled—spoke on earth as heroine after death and walked the Isles of the Blest.

Borderland

Anything could happen here.

In a hidden garden of the Cuyahoga Valley, water plays on chiseled stone. Inside sunken walls, a bronze nymph pours out splashing streams from cupped palms, arms outstretched to make an offering. At her feet, beneath bare winter beds, spirits of spring wait to transform wizened roots, waken artemisia herbs named for their companion, and invite shy nymphs to green the birches. If we choose to see it so. Look where the fountain statue is looking, to where the path ends and nature waits, for those who dare to be vulnerable to the embattled beauty of the forest.

All estate comes to this, ruins found if we wander untethered. Everything at a standstill just north in a vacant quarry. Abandoned for nearly a hundred years, it feels as though the workmen have only just left, and as their footsteps faded, the moss, ivy, and rusty locks unharnessed dominion in an instant. Here is the un-estate. Parmenides said there is no such thing as time passing, no such thing as a later or another time. Or another place. And sometimes, in some places, time does stand still. A kestrel in flight hangs motionless in the air.

Speak, and the moment passes.

A pregnant doe crossed the trail in front of me moments ago, flanks rough and ribs ajar, yet her belly swells gravid from hollowed spaces just behind her breath. Interposed between us, ice-stiffened cattails stripe her coat as she sniffs out acorns, stalk marrow, anything. Seeking sustenance in this late winter matted marsh border where fragile willows drink and the ground rolls up to shoulder oaks. She is matted as the marsh, soaked from icy rain that has just finished pelting everything here. We regard one another, then she continues her search. It is not yet dusk.

Ordinarily she would be lying in her covert this time of day and weather. Maybe she is out because she needs a mouthful of something to survive the cold front coming in. Who knows, maybe she will strip the tiny buds from this slender beech after I am done freeing it from tangling vines. Or maybe not; the crimson points know enough to be bitter. She looks back at me, so still that she could be the fallen tree beside her, if I didn't already know she was there. A hiker treks by with poles and asks, "Do you see something?" I don't give her away. She has already vanished into the bordering trees.

The borderland is the unseen repository for our dreams, our fears, our hopes, our shadow selves. Myths spring up there like weeds; epics grow lofty as trees. We have traveled so long on earth together that deer and cattails know all our myths. Stones with their lichen backs turned away know tales they have not told us yet. Secrets have been whispered into the ground and covered over; earth divulges them one by one, like pale toad-bellies half frozen in spring, or shivered shards of glass.

All is unearthed, slowly, where there is no one to hear. It is a simple piece of projection to accuse the borderland or frontier of being wilder than we are. Anyone might guess this from the valleys and abysses of our dreams. The self-protective myth-generating nature of forests and dreams reveal why Aristotle said that poetic imagination is more stimulating than prosaic history. A mythic story (supposedly) never actually happened, so it is free to happen to anyone, anytime, anywhere. Periphery counters illusions. There dwell rare beauties, and weedy homely things, like ragweed, pokeweed, or poison ivy. We know where their kind grow. Borderland doesn't work according to plan; some gnarled root is always getting in the way. In the way of what? Mythic questions never have a single answer. We move between the everyday world of well-worn *mes* and borderland that doesn't recognize us, to come to know who we are. Here brooks follow their whims, and all our stories began. Marginal territories abound in weedy resources core territories do not possess. These resources are not only material. In fact, their most potent riches are in the imagination. The borderland is the frontier of the imagination, a place where myths take shape, and fade or thrive like statues of gods. Myth from the edge can transform atrophied life at the center. Secretly we glance sideways and look to the margins for meaning.

A forest, real or mythical, invites us to face more than one way, to meet the beings who stalk our dreams. Those who find this dynamic place may live a double life: wild and urbane, mythical and unmythical. If we manage a synthesis, Iris is a rainbow *and* a goddess whose wings refract iridescent light. Rosy-fingered Dawn is also our star, the sun. Both faces are required of humanity now, co-existent and simultaneous, ways of living out and describing practical and mystical experience. We are bilingual as the performers of *Emesal* were, humans with Enki-confounded tongues.

Here in not-paradise, the un-estate, the unlocated scraggly margins, where the possum curls to sleep and the stag leaps the fence, mulberry, hawthorn, and bloodwort hold sway. Here in the remaining habitat of Ninhursag and Artemis, samara who settle are not be mowed down; they live and die on their own terms. Artemis roamed out there in many guises. For an isolated traveler, she scouted narrow passages as "the lookout" and revealed hazardous footing as "torchbearer." On frontiers she was hailed as a savior, "she who turns the enemy back." Human settlements carved into landscapes, and mistresses of wilderness ruthlessly oppose that carving. From a city point of view, wild goddesses roam fluidly in a place that could be best called *not here*. They cherish mysterious spaces that belong to no one. Invisible to straight ways, found only by wending and winding in mythic margins. Remembering the stone seal Inanna wore, we might say that borderland is inscribed on the seal of heaven and earth. Anything can happen where myth emerges, flourishes, and hides.

When we try to examine the borderland, like Eros, it escapes. Over time, as more and more land became fixed into estate, borderland became defined as no place.

A neglected place. Neglected to exist. A place that relies on being forgotten.

Vanished gardens above the spring. Beechdrops. Mayapple circle.
This path doesn't go anywhere. It goes to a place where there is no more path.

The borderland is not on any map. It is where Humbaba dwells content with his trees, the goddess flies with owls on her wings, flood sages keep watch, and Odysseus sleeps beside the double cave. A mythic place intersecting with our everyday existence, intertwined with it yet largely invisible, where a connection with nature is honored as foundational for the flourishing of all beings. The borderland is a mode of enchantment to be found in a real, beloved landscape over the course of long knowing. Those who discover enchantment, whether born to it, beckoned, or led, know that apart from the flourishing of borderland—where invasive approaches avail nothing—all human plans wither away. Perhaps the entrance to this place is through the portal one ancient map captioned as the "gate of unclean women," or the door to Inanna's date storage house, full or empty. Places of grim necessity and shimmering delight, each lived out as fully as we can manage. In forest, waking dream, and myth, we move between.

Does such passage sound easy? I don't know a single myth where things are easy.

Myth is nobody's tool—and anyway, our tools outwit us. As possessions go, myths are Sumerian harp strings that blow away the moment they are lifted from the ground. In some invisible process of fading, in some rationalizing and demythologizing wind, ancient myth has scattered and all but disappeared. Meanwhile, the forest has silently moved apart from us, in a parallel slipping away from common experience and awareness. *Mythago Wood*, as the novelist called it, forest and myth moving together.

The hidden harmony is stronger than the obvious one.
(Heraclitus)

So is the hidden land.

The Muses of Mount Cithaeron

Prophecies, ever living, crowd around him.
(Oedipus the King)

Oedipus, mythical king of Thebes, looked to a mysterious mountain in the borderland for salvation. When trouble came, he hoped that myth-haunted Mount Cithaeron would save him. Here Artemis turned Actaeon into a stag; here King Pentheus was torn to pieces; here Oedipus himself had been left, exposed as an infant to die.

Cithaeron the mountain of my birth—
that my parents tried to make into my tomb.
(Oedipus the King)

The mountain rises today from a plain in central Greece. As horror builds in his suspenseful tragedy, *Oedipus the King*, he calls upon the mountain who nursed him to remember him. The chorus implores the female spirits who dwell there to help them understand the feral crimes that began his story. No one knows the spirits' names.

Actors on the tragic stage, they cannot chant their lines alone. In bewilderment and dread, they look to the unknown goddesses who roam the slopes, and make guesses about their king's birth, so shrouded in mystery. Maybe Oedipus was born on the mountain to a nymph who drew near the goat god Pan, the fertile god of borderland who is both animal and divine. Or maybe he was born to a Muse, who met Apollo "the oblique" or "the obscure" in some cliffside meadow. Nobody is sure, and anyway both guesses are wrong.

The Muses were maidens of many, many songs. With so many compositions to choose from, contradiction could hardly

130

be absent from poetry. Perhaps the Muses taught Oedipus poetic irony in the infant hours he laid upon the mountain. He would need to relish it one day.

Changeability was a divine and perilous quality that always permeated song. Fickleness was freshly noted in writing as soon as writing extended to poetry. Tricksters were specialists, virtuosos in word-craft, where every unit was protean like themselves. Gilgamesh deceives the cedar guardian with hollow oaths; Oedipus unravels the Sphinx through riddles; Prometheus intuits the intricate plans of Zeus. We could go on. Odysseus entices in words that drip honey; the lyre Achilles plays is the artfully tuned trophy of a man he killed; Enki tunes contextual candor to finely deserved degrees.

In a piece of wishful thinking, Enki was hailed as "truthful with those who truth, and false to those who told falsehoods." But what god would agree to that contract? Certainly not him. The acclamation tries to declare him constant or consistent.

The Muses saw early on that language put into writing was in bondage. The word had to be set free from tribute tablets, from bowing down with dusty mouth, from becoming a rack of counting and a bureaucratic king-list. Poetry had to come into being in song and memory too.

And long before that, we have heard a primeval sage warn, from his mouth half-man-half-fish, that one day words would shake off the shackles of meaning. Like Melusine, they would cease to do the work of human imagination and become free to exist as their original selves.

But maybe meaning would stay with us if words could be enticed with beautiful truth. Perhaps, so long as they are honored, meaning is as natural to words as nymphs are natural to springs and trees. Those are guesses. Art does not fit ledgers. Predictability was a species of constraint no mountain-sprung Muse ever offered to a poet. But when they first appeared, the Muses did promise to leave mortals spellbound. It is good to remember that singers began archaic songs by stepping out of their way: Muses sang poetry, not humans. Humans could only sing if the Muses sang through them. These nine daughters of Memory enthralled listeners and made the halls of Zeus ring with their joyful petal-smooth voices. They could:

make men forget their burdens and grant them rest from all their cares,

but only when they wanted to. These enchanting and capricious artists, whose gifts for those they loved included harmonious beauty and creative inspiration, sang so sweetly that a disturbing aspect of their craft might pass unnoticed:

We know many lies and we can make them sound exactly like the truth.
We know also — whenever we wish — how to reveal the actual truth.
Mortals will need our favor to tell the difference.
(Theogony)

Their candid declarations make no contract. They lack any desired symmetry or optimistic *quid pro quo*, leaving every advantage in the Muses' hands. Divine Harmony was the daughter of Aphrodite and Ares, Love and War, after all. Muses could inflict blindness or amnesia; they are adept at the power of *lanthanein*, the ways that nature loves to hide. Accustomed to more mystical companions, the Muses call the mortals who witness their epiphany "rustics and mere bellies." They knew better than to come close; many tried to snare them from the beginning. But they never did perform on demand. As the embodiments of artistic inspiration, they could not be tamed to appear without duplicity or — since they form a chorus — plurality.

They are cousins to the Sirens, who effortlessly and sweetly sang men to their doom. When they so wished. As the Sirens beguilingly hinted, they knew everything that happened on the face of the earth, past, present, and future. Bones of sailors who stopped to hear their song littered the beach at their feet.

But the Muses are not grisly; they are surpassingly beautiful sisters who share many features with capricious nymphs. They offered the blossoming laurel branch of poetry to whomever they chose. They did not choose Oedipus until he was stripped of kingship and looking for a place to die. He would understand Muse-like waywardness, epiphanies, and sudden divine departures, not at the beginning of this play, but at the end.

Behold Oedipus, a king who unraveled legendary riddles,
a man who was most in control—
see how waves of misfortune drag him under.
(Oedipus the King)

His tragedy and eventual redemption could be seen as a journey away from the Muses and back again; always circling the inspiration of prophetic utterance, always circling his own word slips, fencing with word embroidery, word multiplicity, and fleeting insights that will not stay. Caught in the net of what cannot possibly be true, between the wildness of myth and the gatekeeping of the city.

The chorus of city councilors sing of the unknown murderer of their previous king. Oblivious to the murderer's identity, they wonder what such a man would be like. Perhaps—

savage forests and caverns are where the killer lurks,
a lost bull wandering rugged slopes.
He must be desperate, aimless with a misguided foot,
put asunder from the remedy of oracles.
(Oedipus the King)

But Oedipus, standing right beside them listening, is the murderer of his father the previous king, and is far more savage than anyone knows. Through the power of the Muses, the lost bull who lurks in the mountains turns out to be Oedipus too.

He thought he was the ultimate urban man, champion of his city. In truth, he is its scapegoat.

In archaic stories, the voice of forgotten deeds often comes from a scapegoat figure: the one who is youngest, worthless, disfigured, disowned, or cast away. How could a king be that?

In a rite of passage, mud to obliterate former identity might be smeared all over an initiate's face and body, and then washed away to reveal new birth.

Earthy smears of ritual represented slippery birth canals, slimy embankments, or whatever is unseen or rejected by society. Not only exiles and outliers, but anyone who failed, including those who failed to complete rites of transition. Eyeing the list of rejects as I walk the banks of the muddy Cuyahoga, I wonder who on earth would be left to belong anywhere. And anyway, all the time we are drawing definitions and boundaries, making insiders and outsiders, the goddess of the underworld is crying "My pain is inside, my pain is outside," because inside and outside flow one and the same. As for the definitions and divisions we make, or Oedipus is panicked to make, the slightest current sheds them with ease. We reach into water and water erases our hand.

Oedipus is learning these things.

His model for looking outside city walls to a mountain in the borderland may have been Humbaba, who was fostered by a mountain. Or it may have the legendary Titan Prometheus, the protagonist in the older tragedy *Prometheus Bound*. In that play, the primeval god of prophecy and foreknowledge is outcast.

For his merciful disposition and illicit gifts to humans, Prometheus was nailed as a malefactor to steep crags in the remote wilderness of the Caucasus mountain range. As he stands in chains, an eagle of mammoth wingspan swoops down on him every day and greedily pecks at his liver. Once Zeus had planned to blot out humanity and create a more docile version; Prometheus alone opposed him. He stole fire from Zeus for the sake of shivering humans: the gift *Homo erectus* accepted over a million years ago to survive. Now, bound alone on a bleak precipice, Prometheus is supposed to learn to fear the highest Olympian god.

The archetypal conflict springs from Zeus's deadly fear of — and desire for — whatever eludes his grasp. He swallowed Metis, the goddess of clever wisdom when he met her, to imprison her wily power and channel it for himself. Now he seeks to transfix Prometheus, the god of foreknowing, with inextricable bonds, adamantine shackles hammered into mountainside. As a sky god, Zeus wields the thunderbolt, the shaft he uses to transfix. Prometheus, however, is a Titan so primeval that from his perspective and genealogy, all Olympian gods seem juvenile. Like Lilith, he is dissident. For refusing to bow down, he stands spreadeagled to freeze in winter and roast in summer, in steadfast opposition to Zeus's rule.

Where is he standing in chains? In the Greek imagination, the Caucasus was borderland, the remote edge of the world. We have glimpsed that region of forest and myth. The place defined, as Zeus seeks to define Prometheus, as the place we turn our backs on. But like a Titan, borderland weathers rejection — or even requires it. The periphery grows its own protection and wears more than one face.

Divine advisers, seconds-in-command, are recognized in Mesopotamian art by their double faces. Diplomats, enforcers, factotums, or couriers, they face more than one way, and are sometimes more astute and powerful than their supposed betters. From the edge of the world, Prometheus sees centers of power with greater clarity than Zeus or Oedipus can muster.

He is a liminal prophet in a pivotal place—out on the periphery of myth.

The Titan who stole fire from heaven was meant to "stand in vigil on a loveless rock" for circling years, ages, and eons, threatened with empty silence while he hears no voice but his own. But in his tragedy, when he cries out, the sacred landscape answers with compassion. He finds kinship with Earth, stars, and a goddess who strays across the stage, wandering the world as a fellow-victim of Zeus. A chorus of daughters of Oceanus also approach the desolate mountain to comfort him. Then they stay, determined to share his fate. Even at the end of the action, when the thunderbolt of Zeus is about to strike Prometheus, and the ground begins to rumble, the wind-winged Oceanids cling to the rocks and stay by his side.

Do not tell us to betray him like cowards!
We hear the thunder gathering in the distance.
We will not flee the deafening bellow of Zeus.
We will endure with Prometheus whatever he must endure.
(Prometheus Bound)

Meant to stand alone in silence for ten thousand years, Prometheus is not alone, and not silenced. During his last moments in the light of the sun for generations to come, before Zeus casts him headlong into the lowest pit of Tartarus, the region of darkness far beneath Hades, Prometheus calls upon his mother Themis. She is an earth goddess of clear counsel.

My mother, who shares one body with Earth,
who is known by many names,
prophesied to me how all would come to pass.

O bright purity of constellations,
freedom of winds on distant wings,

springs who give birth to rivers that flow away,
waves who run infinite, laughing in the sea,
Mother Earth and circling sun who sees all, behold.

Witness what I suffer, a god at the mercy of gods.
(Prometheus Bound)

His mother Themis is the prophetic goddess of inevitable natural law. Her justice is rooted into the earth and woven into the fabric of tides and constellations. She hears her son.

The laws of the goddess Justice need no words.
Therefore, they are secure.
Not for today or yesterday,
they live forever.
No one except Themis knows when Justice was born.
Hate she has never understood. She manifests where there is love.
(Antigone)

Prometheus Bound came first in a trilogy. The other two tragedies were long ago lost. But we know the last play's title: *Prometheus Unbound.*

Never Let This City Hold Me

Never let this city hold me,
inhabiting any home.
Let me live among the mountains, on Cithaeron.
(Oedipus the King)

Once Oedipus unravels the mystery of his own myth, the only place he has left to go is into the wasteland. He goes as a pauper. Out there, he is destined for a life of wandering like the mountain bull, in the wilderness where he was meant to die as an infant only days old. To this desolation he must return for his healing, full circle. The renowned king, the triumphant city man, expected to build a lifetime of splendid achievements.

Then fate tore up all his civic plans.

No hero can name his quest when words will not stay fixed, omens keep shifting sideways, and he cannot even understand his own name. In his tragic journey through *Oedipus the King*, Oedipus moved in self-concept from champion of truth to exiled scapegoat, and as he went, he found that words, capricious as Muses or Sirens, refused to stay fixed. Names, titles, places, times, singulars, plurals, and kinships all refuse to be defined; they all keep turning out to mean their opposite. In such confusion of labeling, numbering, and categorization, he undertakes to investigate the murder of his father, the very crime that Oedipus himself unwittingly committed long ago. He grasps at straws:

"The eyewitness claimed that a band of robbers killed Laius—
several men.
Unless he changes his story, I could not be the killer—I am one man.
It is impossible for one man to be many."
(Oedipus the King)

Or is it? One man does turn out to be singular enough to be the same as many. Oedipus's role as husband turns out to be one with his role as son, since Iokasta—his queen, his wife, and the mother of his children—is one and the same as his own birth mother. His multiple yet single role as king, husband and son brings pollution upon his city. In the realm of the Muses, words slip, rumors whisper, reports emerge from secrets long suppressed, and all will be revealed. A murky truth begins to take shape.

Oedipus is one man in the city and another in the borderland, and the two have never met.

In his desperation, Oedipus' self-concept becomes circular and wild. He imagines himself living out beyond the city, a child of nature, not of man, out where the Muses sing on the goddess-haunted mountain of Cithaeron. There in his fantasy, mountain nymphs might have nursed him as a child; perhaps they will succor him again.

When Aphrodite herself once thought to abandon a child, she had a similar plan:

As soon as the child is born and looks on the light of the sun, compassionate nymphs who dwell on sacred peaks will nurture him.
(Homeric Hymn to Aphrodite)

In the alternative story Oedipus is forging, his civic and social identities crumble. Perhaps he does not take after mortals, but nymphs. In his fantastic searching for a new self, he sees the mountain as his original, true mother. He begs:

Let me go. Let me live among the mountains, on Cithaeron.
(Oedipus the King)

He was not born on the mountain; he was exposed there as

an infant to die. But it was on those slopes that he uncannily survived and was reborn. His origins begin to come to light.

On Mount Cithaeron, in a cleft ravine of woodland, you were found.
(Oedipus the King)

The Muse beloved mountain begins to dominate and haunt his memory and vision. So does another place in his memory. The narrow chasm where he encountered a prophetess of exotic form: the half woman, half winged lioness, the Sphinx.

Years before, when the young Oedipus was forging ahead in his persona as champion of truth, the unfamiliar path to Thebes narrowed down to a strangulation, a fateful passage. Not only once, but twice. First at the place where Oedipus killed his father —

O triple crossroads and hidden vale,
coppice of oak and the narrow path
at the place where three roads meet —
(Oedipus the King)

and then again where the road constricted at the valley of the Sphinx, whom he remembers as "Cruel Singer." Her name means something closer to "strangler." When she opens her throat to speak riddles, she nooses others' fates. Like the Muses, she is an intuitive untamed singer who never appears onstage, but her perceptive melodies drive the tragic plot. For the lone traveler Oedipus who was taking the unknown road between named places, a single unforeseen spot narrowed to become a knot, a nexus, a convergence, a confluence, a destiny.

Then opened out again.

Once Oedipus's grip on royal dynasty is torn away and he becomes blind, his inward vision turns away from the palace toward the periphery. Now in new-forged relationship, he directly addresses the mountain:

Why, Cithaeron? Why did you receive me?
Why did you not kill me straightaway?
(Oedipus the King)

To understand Oedipus now, the chorus turns with him to face the mountain, whose rocky slopes loomed in the distance beyond the stage. They hope that its cliffs or native nymphs will offer some insight, some clue, about their formerly civilized king, newly exposed as feral in origin and *arkhē*.

Who was it who bore you, child Oedipus?
One of the blessed nymphs?
Did she draw near Pan, god of deserted hills?
Mount Cithaeron, Oedipus reveres you,
as his native earth, nurturer, and mother.
(Oedipus the King)

Like Oedipus, they will do anything, engage in any fantasy, to avoid the true name of his mother.

The trouble is, as Oedipus optimistically says early on:

If we reveal even a slender hope,
uncover a single hidden clue,
one investigation will lead to many insights.
(Oedipus the King)

Aspiration is his undoing. The cost of truth will be paid not only with Oedipus's eyes. By the end of the play, all his consequences come due, to be paid for with permanent exile from human community. It will also be settled in the currency of others' lives. Many in his city died from the plague his pollution caused. The

141

Sphinx threw herself over a cliff when he untied her riddle. Once Iocasta learns that she has loosened her sash for her own son, and the enigma of her exposed infant is solved, the strangling theme returns. She silences herself in her private chamber with textiles knotted into a noose. We learn that Oedipus has never won anything from his supposed triumphs.

When a flashlight beam is narrowed, it suddenly illuminates more brilliantly. But first it requires darkness all around.

In the tragic world of Oedipus, what the Muses of Mount Cithaeron illuminate is the fear of terrible discovery—discovery of the truth. And such discovery lives in sacred landscapes. Primal ferocity and human terror are depths that Sirens and Sphinxes sport in. It is their very playground. Not so for Oedipus, the iconic civilized man undone. If he were reasonable, he might fear divine reprisals in the wasteland. But he is not reasonable anymore.

The fear of Oedipus lives in civilized vision that, entranced by custom and convention, forgets what is owed to savage landscapes. Denies the radical horror of the unknown to be cocooned in civilized identity. Nature is crippling, armed with plague, noose, and riddles. She will not be denied. The way becomes too narrow. Wild crags and wild goddesses will speak whether we want them to or not. Oedipus is driven out of his city into the uncultivated borderland. Yet once he is powerless, he is empowered to enter that landscape in truth—naked and bowed down. Blind, surrendered, broken. In fulfillment of his mountain fantasy, he does become a mountain wanderer, a man who is at home no place, his footsteps crossing nymph-inhabited, Muse-haunted trackless land.

But his journey does not end there.

Often *Oedipus the King* is known apart from Sophocles' last tragedy *Oedipus at Colonus*. That oversight leaves us mid-story with the well-known image of the bloody-eyed king in despair. But for his final play, Oedipus changed his mask. He is an old man now. His indelible scars and wounds of *kharaktēr* are changing, and are about to be utterly healed. When the two stories are put together, they reveal the *katabasis* of a king who survives the social tragedy of exile and experiences the spiritual liberation of going feral. Only then does the deposed and despised scapegoat emerge to become the protector of, and to be protected by, a fiercely beautiful plot of sacred land.

Cast out of all cities, far from any home, the exhausted beggar Oedipus finally stops in an unfamiliar forest grove. Close to death, he can go no further. The place he has stumbled on is honored by Muses and nymphs and sheltered by great goddesses and gods. This lushly watered, flowering place is where the exiled wanderer ends his journey. Since he is blind, the chorus describes the sacred landscape for him. It is no wasteland. But it is not a paradise either, for the land around is torn by war; Erinyes, female spirits of curse and vengeance, guard the site. Oedipus knows he has earned both curse and revenge.

Why would Erinyes shelter the beggar they cursed when he was a king?

Oedipus's pollution brought an epidemic down on his entire city. In ancient Greek thought, certain crimes, such as the patricide and incest of Oedipus, caused *miasma*, religious blight that could emerge in natural phenomena such as disease. He is represented in ancient sources as ignorant of his sacrilegious deeds (not, like modern polluters, aware of impact and hoping to escape the natural consequences). To use a watercourse metaphor, Oedipus is a man whose offenses sickened everyone who lived downstream. To use a mythic metaphor, he is a sojourner through withdrawal and devastation who will never experience return.

Yet in the end, the hero who lost everything, the destitute exile, finds refuge in a sacred grove that welcomes him. Committing his body to this land, he is transfigured into its guardian spirit, a watchful hero who will walk here forever. His mythic return from devastation could never aim toward home, so it moves toward peace that he had never experienced before, for all his status, wealth, and power. The chorus sings for the man who has been an outsider from birth, no matter what city he tried to inhabit. They describe the garden of Colonus, his final, unhoped-for refuge.

Stranger, understand where you have come.
Freely the nightingale trills blithe melodies here.
She warbles in wooded glens, nestling in deep ivy
and dusky foliage abundant with berries.
She is sheltered here from heat,
safeguarded from windstorms,
weaving her nest inviolate
in a place beloved by immortals.

The god of wine dances here
thronged by the nymphs who nurtured him.

Safely flourishes the lustrous narcissus here,
fed by celestial dew, ever fresh,
opening fragrant blooms by day,
for garlands worn only by goddesses,
twined with crocus gleaming gold.
Springs meander here and there,
cool waters brim pure, and do not fail.
Ever renewing, the river with gentle current
soothes the tranquil nesting of this land.
(Oedipus at Colonus)

Then they give the clue that aged Oedipus, near death, searching for his final resting place, longs to hear.

This country is haunted by gatherings of the Muses.
(Oedipus at Colonus)

Colonus is a vision of the healing wild, salvation-by-borderland, sought by heroes ever since Gilgamesh left the city of Uruk in search of a sacred landscape. As for Oedipus, in his final moments as king, before they turned him out of the palace, they told him:

Seek no more to master anything.
(Oedipus the King)

Forensic investigation, human-muddled prophecy, and masterful action could not save Oedipus. A nightingale did.

Oedipus the infant of ill omens barely survived his first few days of life, stolen away to die exposed on wild Cithaeron. Oedipus the king grew into a man of prowess; monsters, households, and governments yielded to his skillful word. Oedipus the exile, limping, straying, done with arguments, lays down his homeless life among streams and crocuses, Muses, and nightingales. He lays down all power and self-determination. He lays down the city for a vision of mystical refuge. And the watchful spirits who dwell in this ground lay down their vengeance to honor his grave.

Staff of Laurel, Staff of Ash

One staff is alive, the other is not. Or so it seems. Let them speak for dynamic opposites in myth.

The first staff blossoms with laurel, a living gift from the Muses to archaic poets. The second is a battle-earned artifact brandished by archaic warriors. It is made of ash. As limbs or artifacts from trees, wooden staffs, rods, and scepters were meant to confer the resilience of trunks and throb of sap to the rising voice of speakers. That was their function. But did they obey?

Because ancient specimens have emerged from excavations, archaeology joins myth once more. The staffs of laurel and ash come face to face and will allow us to learn their characters, to awaken, warn and inspire. Their dialectic has been running beneath this story all along. Ancient voices in the sacred landscape, the questions they raise are timely and pressing.

We have seen all along that when humans first began to irrigate, plow, cut timber, mine for metals, and domesticate other species, anxiety about these projects emerged in the intensely alive and sacred songs of myth. In a world alive with the intelligence of nature, anxiety-inducing projects and objects lived their own lives and talked back. Their concerns are what we have been listening for: the first ecological conversations, couched in archaic myths about protecting or ravaging the environment. In those stories, our desires—and our ambivalence about forcing the land to serve our desires—first engaged the earth in ongoing dialogue.

This is the dialogue between the two staffs.

Mesopotamian audiences delighted in spirited mythical debates. Turtle debated heron; sheep disputed grain; bird contested fish; hoe argued with plow. Millstone contended with raw rock. Summer and winter, silver and copper, date palm and tamarisk, all competed to win. A suspenseful outcome was part of the drama. But when we turn to the staffs of laurel and ash, it seems that we already know, or fear that we might know, the winner.

But let's not assume the ending yet. Archaic poets found both staffs glorious and disturbing. They come from times and places where humans were miniscule and striving to survive. Who would have wagered on the persistence of our species against vast humbling vistas? We felt small beneath all we surveyed.

Earth is ageless, plows will never weary her.
(Antigone)

The sea is right there, who could ever exhaust its resources?
(Agamemnon)

These confident voices speak from days when most mortals never dreamed that we might drain the sea of fish or deplete the earth's topsoil. Or ever trouble the entire living organism some have returned to calling Gaia.

Earth or Gaia was there at the beginning of Greek myth when she emerged from primeval Chaos to birth mountains, sea, and sky. How could any mortal hope to fittingly honor or describe her? The answer is that no one could hope to, not on their own. But fortunately, one night, some shepherds were drowsing near their flocks, when mysterious goddesses descended from sacred groves on the lofty snowcapped peaks. Dancing, singing, arousing, and enchanting, they appeared out of the mist. They brought with them the gift of song.

On the peak of Mount Helicon
they dance on delicate feet
to circle the fresh spring wreathed in violets
and the altar of vigorous Zeus.
They bathe their supple limbs in numinous pools,

fountains and springs where divinity's presence is felt.
Secluded, they entwine together in lovely dances,
and the rhythm of their feet awakens desire.
Then from the mountain's crest they drift down,
concealed by night, swathed in veils of mist,
and arrive all unseen to lift entrancing voices.
(Theogony)

These are sisters to the Muses so beloved of Oedipus, who move from spring to spring and mountain to mountain, in mindful harmony of their own making. While Oedipus imagined them only from afar, they appeared directly to the shepherd Hesiod. This epiphany, mantled in mystery, mist, and longing, was on Mount Helicon, a mountain known in myth as the Muse-haunted brother of Mount Cithaeron. Before the elusive Muses vanished, they left the shepherd enraptured with something to hold, a tangible gift. That night on themountain:

They gave to me a staff of luxuriantly blossoming laurel,
a branch they plucked from a laurel tree flushed with blooms,
a divine staff—a thing of wonder. Then they breathed into me
a voice that could sing what a god would sing
or say what a branch of laurel would say,
so that I would make known true myths
of things that once had been, and things still yet to come.
They commanded me to compose hymns for all the immortals,
but always with the Muses to begin and end my songs.
(Theogony)

Now, as nympholept, Hesiod could speak not just words, but the peculiar language of myth. This mattered. Let us not forget what writing sounded like on most ancient tablets:

For the palace: tribute: 50 rams, incense of juniper.

For the citadel: supplies: spindles, pestles, wagon wheels.
To the leather makers: grain, wine, figs.
To the flax-spinners: one jar of olive oil and a weight of wool each.
140 unpaid workers of Samos.
60 contracted laborers from Uruk.
20 captive weavers brought to Pylos: 12 with children.
165 pack mules.
It has been recorded, and I have copied it out.

But then the Muses touched the mouths of poets and scribes with honey, and liberated words from the enslavement of official bookkeeping. The staff of laurel brought this gift to Greece; in Mesopotamia it must have been a branch from Cedar Mountain. Divine song is a honeyed, subtle, and sobering gift. Muses effortlessly mingle lies with truth and sort them out again; they impart only as much as they think human listeners can handle. They impeccably perceive the past and future. In contrast, mortals often miss the obvious and respond to robust problems from puny perspectives. The Muses warn Hesiod to guard the staff by remembering he is only human: "Know thyself," as Apollo of Delphi commanded. Hesiod is transformed into a poet—but an ephemeral creature will never be a Muse. Failing conscientious use of myth, the blessing of divine song could always be taken away again, as Enki once did with the *mes*. After deriding the shepherds as mere bellies to encourage humility, the Muses hand over the branch. It is a moment of crisis. The mellifluous persuasion of myth is being granted to such a fallible species, one with such ravenous appetites.

Appetites for what? Seemingly, for everything in earth, sea, and sky.

Gastēr in Ancient Greek means stomach (as in gastric), desire, appetite, even gluttony. This is the Muses' unflattering nickname for a mortal: a belly. It was a vital word in ethics. Ethically speaking, the belly was a metaphor for appetite, for any desire that overwhelms. For humans, this means knowing the right but doing wrong anyway. Wanting too much. Demanding too much from the natural world.

What a risk the Muses took to bring myth to creatures of appetite, with lives as transient as the lives of leaves. Apollo questioned why gods should bother:

passionate but capable of only slight things,
mortals eat what fruit they labor for,
then wither away, heartless.
(Iliad)

But because the goddesses gambled on humans, something extraordinary happened.

Now an artist could speak in myth. Not necessarily compose it at first, but a listener captivated around the fire could appreciate a good story and pass it on later with a flourish. Myth is language to be savored: intensely alive and free, told in a sacred way, with *melam* and sometimes even *hili*. In a sense, the Muses brought the opening of the mouth ritual to Hesiod with animated song.

Hesiod's specialty as a poet of creation myth was to sing *arkhē*: the birth of the gods.

That night on Mount Helicon was a thousand years before Apollo's oracle was silenced.

When mortals affronted the earth, Muse-inspired archaic poets made sure that oaks cried out for justice, rivers expressed outrage, and streams lamented in story. When rulers oppressed their subjects, poets made sure to sing about hawks who were cruel to nightingales, war campaigns between primeval elements, and gods who deposed their greedy fathers in violent coups. Devotion to the sprig of laurel challenged top-heavy appetites for resource greed, aggressive dominion, and warfare. Such myths traveled with conquerors, but not for their comfort. But such stories were heard in nurseries and mountain hovels with delight. And they sprang up to startle the ethical imagination even of kings and queens.

Neck turned, looking straight at the viewer, at any moment the limestone temple calf with etched pupils, arched eyebrows, and bent foreleg is about to rise.

Once we hear myths with an ear for environmental concerns, protean stories submerge and surface to reveal the unfamiliar inside the familiar. They are free to dive anywhere they wish, and they do. Nobody asks, Is this tale really about a hawk or a nightingale? From childhood we know the answer is yes. Hawk, nightingale, ogre, dog-groin, and hundred-handed giant animate all they touch. In mythic song, our *mes*, our furrows, wells, oaths, and foundations, stand up for or against us and speak. So do harps, axes, storage jars, hair ribbons, inscribed stone seals, and staffs.

Tales will always continue to slip in where logic cannot go. In faltering ecosystems, myth might become a resonant call for action. It has been this way since the blooming laurel talisman made it so.

Even though he was only a belly, Hesiod was certain that Earth expressed herself, that she was alive and teemed with divinities. When the Muses speak through archaic songs, they reveal what is honored when humans honor what is wild, and what is lost when the earth is mistreated or ruthlessly pursued. The monster covered in shaggy bark and the water sprite holding a golden comb say, Protect cedar, Honor water. But how plain. Muses say it far more strangely than that. If we hesitate to voice such issues, Earth finds ways to raise the laurel staff and speak. She is ecologically eloquent.

In the natural transformation of myth, the staff of laurel has turned out to be a branch. Now we will turn to the staff of ash. It doesn't shimmer, it doesn't swell with sap. It will turn out to be a spear.

At the opening of the *Iliad*, a staff appears in the hand of the Greeks' greatest warrior, Achilles. He doesn't merely hold it. His thoughts grow distant as he dwells on its details:

> *I will speak out, and swear a great oath,*
> *by this staff I hold in my hand—*
> *a staff that will nevermore sprout leaves or stems,*
> *now that it has left behind forever*
> *its severed trunk in the mountains.*
> *It will never blossom again, a fate made certain*
> *once the bronze axe stripped away its living foliage*
> *and carved off its protective bark.*
> *Now in its final place, the sons of the Achaeans take it,*
> *as a tool of justice in their hands when they issue laws of Zeus.*
> (Iliad)

It fascinates Achilles so much that his sentence wanders, and no wonder. It is a tool of chilling significance. We see that it is bare. A bronze blade has stripped it. "Stripped" is a battle word in the *Iliad*, as in "he stripped the life from him" or "stripped the armor from his corpse for a trophy." This is the vulnerability of Inanna naked in the Great Below. This staff is no laurel branch that resembles its tree, but a wooden status symbol. It is emphatically dead. It will never leaf out or blossom again, and war chiefs seize it to solidify dominant positions. Although this staff grants the power to be heard, it is no gift, but a riveting object passed from hand to hand as speakers gain and lose ascendancy in the crowd. Nothing could be further from the staff of everblooming laurel.

Hesiod's laurel branch, with its misty mountain legend, comes from the *Laurus nobilis*, a native species recognizable by blossom and leaf since it grew in the familiar landscape where the Muses first appeared. But the staff of ash is severed from its local roots. Invaders carried it far from home to the siege encampment of Troy. It arrives to serve the powerful and to lend eloquence to kings as they divide the spoils of war. When a disabled, lowly foot soldier dares to speak out in assembly, it does not matter that he is telling the truth; Odysseus beats him with this staff.

Achilles holds it in assembly. In battle, he wields another kind of staff: an heirloom spear made from a tree of ash, passed down from his paternal line, that no one else dare touch. Surveying these tools of mastery, we remember the construction tool that was a corpse-devouring snake; we see Assyrian royal statues holding sickle sword and scepter; and pharaohs wielding the mace. Beyond the desire to dominate, the heroic quest for immortality speaks from the staff of ash. The ash-handled spear of Achilles is his tool to survive by making others die.

Immortal fame can be won by spearing opponents. In the *Iliad*, the perfect undying fame that heroes hungered and died for is literally called "not-withering." Strange. Nothing alive inhabits that state for long. But ironically, one way to stop something from withering is to remove its withering parts. To strip it down to a stick and set it free from seasonal change. When Achilles is set loose upon a battlefield holding his grandfather's wooden spear of ash, he is a warrior who has been stripped of mercy. What is left alive in him? Absorbed in killing, he is seeking unwilting immortality. As Gilgamesh desired on Cedar Mountain:

A name to live forever I will establish.
(Epic of Gilgamesh)

Surely such uncompassionate unwithering is the opposite of life. But myth always reveals its opposite.

In myth, the severed head of the mythic poet Orpheus sang on. In myth, imprisoned waters long for their riverbeds; an arrow flies eager to bite its target, and the vibration of a drum resonates like the sheen of a young man's strength. A stone statue is inanimate, but suddenly animate. A tree is mute until she speaks. Foreheads and loincloths radiate luminous auras. So maybe Achilles emphasized the ash staff's deadness because of his own impending death. Its unwithering leafless and rootless homeless state would then be his. Poets do still sing about Achilles; his song has not withered away.

Staffs have more life in them than we think—in myth.

Without myth, we imagine they are wooden and forget the roots where they were born.

Far from his homeland, Achilles in the *Iliad* is about to die. We need to return to the *arkhē* of Achilles. If only his origins had remained his guiding principles.

He is the son of silver-footed Thetis, and he calls to her when he is troubled. His sea nymph mother never fails to respond. And other female voices haunt his past, back when he was another man before the war. Andromache, woman of Troy, speaks of a former Achilles who was deadly, who killed her father and brothers. But she remembers that he used to be able to feel pity. She knew him then.

Achilles slew my father but did not dishonor him.
He did not strip him of his armor.
His spirit was moved by respect for his worthy opponent.
Achilles burned him on a pyre,
dressed in all his finely wrought battle gear,
and labored himself to build the mound over his grave.

Surrounding Achilles as he worked,
nymphs came down from their mountains,
lovely daughters of Zeus, and to protect the place,

to grant honor and graceful shade,
they planted a sacred grove of elm trees all around.
(Iliad)

In her memory Achilles is burying her father, a man Achilles killed. As Andromache describes the scene, she sees a glimmer of compassion left in him. The nymphs of his opponent's native mountains, who plant elms for a king they once loved, bear witness to a former, more merciful days. Once upon a time, after battle, Achilles attended the rituals of a nymph-haunted place, to heal the scars he had wrought on the land.

When Achilles himself goes to his death, his mother gathers every nymph in the sea to her watery halls, to lament the fate of the son she had nurtured "like the young tree beloved of its orchard." If we follow clues further back into Achilles' childhood, we find again that he honored nature deities—long ago before Troy.

Just as the staff of ash will never rejoin its splintered stump, Achilles will never return to his home. Like the exile of Oedipus, war is the *katabasis* of Achilles without a journey back. He defines his imminent death not only as a loss of homeland, but specifically as a bond with a river that he grew up beside—a bond he has severed. In his native land, a river god had sworn to protect his rite of passage to manhood, and Achilles had pledged sacrifices in return. Near the end of his life, Achilles calls out to him, asking for understanding, praying to be released from their oaths.

O River Sperkheios, on the day when I came to manhood,
I would have cut my hair for you in sacrifice,
in gratitude for safe passage out of childhood,
in gratitude for safe homecoming out of war.
I would have offered sacrifices for you,
home beside your consecrated springs,

home inside your sanctuary, before your aromatic altar.
(Iliad)

It is only at this moment, as he prepares to light the funeral pyre of his best friend, that we realize how young Achilles is. By then, the *Iliad* is almost over. Achilles asks the river to forgive him for devotion he will never express. He chooses never to flower fully, and never to go back home.

Archaic poetry is luminous with aching beauty and stalked by hideous violence. War is costly. Achilles could not face his guardian river after what he became at Troy. He dies from a dispute with his king over heaped-up spoils of war, treasures that included captives. "Currency-exchanger of corpses" is an archaic name for Ares, the god of the Trojan—and every—war. The *Iliad* foreshadows the imminent fall and sack of a city. Noncombatants stand on the city wall: elders, women, and children. From the very start we face the end, because this is a myth about a tipping point, the gathering doom of an entire civilization. The epic closes with the doom of a landscape too: a picture of days spent felling trees and hauling wood as the besieged Trojans, fearful of renewed attack, gather wood for funeral pyres for their countless dead.

Kingship like the one Achilles died for did not arise for nothing alongside priestly administration, standing military, bureaucracy, domestication, plant monoculture, social stratification, enforced tribute, and recordkeeping technologies. Kingship arose as a fulcrum for new consciousness. In this rising consciousness, truth was no longer the terror behind the savage beauty of Artemis or Inanna, but the masked servant of cunningly worded desires. Such "truth" could move like an engine of war; it could be made new every day.

Flow backward, sacred rivers, wheel about.
Let every custom turn and be reversed.
(Medea)

This *katastrophê* of oppressive kingship could only happen in a community controlled by an entourage who held a staff of ash. A bronze-tipped one, forged by fire and hardened by hammer. To silence voices that spoke uncomfortable truths. Such an entourage needed to control not just one, but both staffs. But who could enslave a laurel blossom?

In the mouth of a speaker holding the ash staff, the truth slid like oil on stone. If necessary, it slid like a cyclopean stone, with captive women and children to oil its path until it fit into the fortress wall. If Shulgi, Ur-Nammu, Naram-Sin, Ashurbanipal, Alexander, or a Caesar wanted to be divine, so it was decreed. If they wished to stand on mountains of enemy corpses skewered with javelins, smite foreigners on the head with maces, hurtle them into monstrous nets, or drive the rope-necked conquered into slavery with pikes, so it was carved in stone. All these images come from ancient victory monuments. And if the next king said those things had not been done, *damnatio memoriae*, take out the chisel again: those things had never been done. So decreed the staff of ash. But the staff of laurel was still blooming.

Though we sometimes forget to link the two, Hesiod knew the Muses had equal care both for creative imagination and for fair justice.

The Muses sing harmonious laws and customs,
raising lovely voices for all the gods and all the world.

If they honor a king and cherish him from birth,
they pour sweet dew onto his tongue
and gentle words flow from his mouth like honey.
People see him determine what is fair,
providing justice clear and candid.
With wisdom he stops a spiteful quarrel.
He brings compassion to the assembly.

A king like this has respect wherever people gather.

He has the sacred gift the Muses gave to humankind.

Blessed are the ones the Muses love.
A honey-sweet voice pours from their lips.
Blessed are those beloved of the Muses:
singers, poets, lyre players, and just kings.
(Theogony)

Straight justice and sweet song are gifts for all humankind. Law, art, and myth flow from honeyed mouth for anyone who has ears to hear. And what is earthy and humble grounds the powerful, though a king of crooked justice might wish to forget it.

Rivers and Earth, stand as witnesses.
Keep watch over our oaths of fidelity.
(Iliad)

The borderland is a mythic place, like the wilderness is a real place, and like the two staffs, they all intersect with our everyday existence, intertwined with us yet largely invisible. They constantly overlap. This overlap is why the *Iliad* weaves earthy images into the work of war: diving fish, crying birds, oxen hungry for home, a poor widow at her loom, a toddler holding her mother's skirts, the forested rivers of our birth. Scenes of home awaken longing for faraway places, places we dream of, where connection with nature is honored as foundational for the flourishing of all of life.

The Muses arrive veiled in mist, and the blooming branch they offer is conditional. Tropism is a force for nonviolence that happens too slow to be seen. But tender roots can heave up the heaviest throne. Hope still clings inside the rim of Pandora's jar.

Inanna hung like rotted meat on an underworld wall. Until she rose again.

Many things the immortal ones
accomplish beyond our knowledge.
What we expect is not fulfilled.
The unexpected comes to pass.
Such is the outcome of this story.
(Medea)

To the staff of ash, we lend our lives. The staff of laurel is already alive. Stories end in unexpected ways. If we look over our shoulder, not only what we threw away as detritus is following us. What we despaired we had lost forever, long ago in the depths of ancient ages, is following us too. We require myth, intensely alive myth, to see it. It is very good at not being seen.

Arborvitae

We began in a row of ancient white oaks along an abandoned carriage road, just north of a stream that feeds the Cuyahoga River. We end in a grove of arborvitae not far away from that spot. Both are sacred landscapes. Ancient poets have led us down winding trails in between, from the axe of Gilgamesh to the gardens of nymphs, toward enigmas cloaked in earth and water, inspiring us to viewing beloved, imperiled places through the wild eyes of ancient myth. The maple seed with its unpredictable descending spiral and a crooked river began our themes of fragmentation and mythic journeys to the underworld. We have excavated a few treasures of darkness: buried stories we meant to go back for, words that say things we no longer can.

Wander in leafy shadows, musing on where to settle in, and the spirit of the hour will find a way to say, here is the place. Today a Northern Flicker alights, treads delicate feet all alert, and considers me from above. Beneath her quickening glance I slowly sit to lean against a mottled cedar trunk.

Within this fragrant precinct, spaded more than a century ago, dawn's tenderest shafts slit the towering dark green vault. Slants of light tremble—the only way to enter this living cave.

Cool water murmurs, dripping through apple
branches, all this sacred grove is shadowed by roses,
and sifting down, from leaves that tremble,
alights deep and dreamless sleep.
(Sappho)

A fossil ammonite was given to me the same year I discovered this arboretum grove. No, the fossil came to me in the same season that this arborvitae threshold opened. This animal in stone is perfectly cupped for an open palm, an elegant, curved companion. On a shelf near a northern-looking window, its spiral protects beloved books and discarded arboretum plaques that once identified trees. The books are worn, and the plaques are too, found scattered half-submerged on the forest floor far from their namesakes. I look down, and a woodlouse pauses to consider the corner of my journal page, rippling shimmering banks of legs. Since the stone-ridged ammonite rippled its legs, how many millions of years have passed? None? It curves back to the place where we began, where every form, living or sleeping, waits.

Inside this leafy screen, within this contemplative circle of trees, I wonder what eon it will be when I step outside again. Outside the grove, will time have passed at all? Arborvitae breaths are prayers that sculpt space and time. If we were forgetful, we might suppose the stately trees form a mere physical assemblage. We might neglect the past, when vows of silence and contemplation came as gifts to humans from the rooted vows of trees. They were our oldest gods.

Emerging from excavations, votive figurines with molded breasts, hands clasped at the waist. Elongated bodies, pillars with flared bases of clay.

Some of the tree goddesses who rise here, flaring skirts of stone and clay above deep rivers of roots, sprout waist-thick branches snaking near enough to the ground to invite rest against their massive shaggy columns streaked with scarlet. Some do not invite.

The grove I sit inside is whole. Woodchip piles not far from this spot signal the felling of larches in stands to the west. Out of the marshland Enki reaches out.

When I first made pilgrimage here decades ago, the eldest arborvitae in the heart of the grove appeared unitary, almost solitary in dignity among daughters. Years later, she gestures beyond herself toward the entire grove, its quickness and slowness, its births, rottings, rettings, and saps, its raccoon excrement and slug trails, its coiled tracks of beetle larvae nosing under bark in slowly traced hieroglyphs beyond our ken. Its protections and vulnerabilities. Infinite divinity graces this aromatic soil and makes it fertile; every moment, every crunching step, every glance of a bird is revelation. Needles shed in seasons past blanket the spongy forest floor in crisscross patterns. All speaks, and all is silent.

Ancient philosophers who mused about natural elements intuited early on that nothing could come from nothing. And that nothing could be destroyed either. Some wondered about invisible indestructible elements that were mixed throughout the cosmos. Like spirits, the elements whirled, united, separated, and remixed. These ingredients of everything-in-everything were everywhere, in constant motion, and infused with intelligence. Anaxagoras called them seeds. Wise and restless seeds return us to maple tree samaras. There is divine intelligence, appearing in infinite forms, in everything.

In accordance with a vow, I have come to this domain beyond the clutch of words, the rarely-pilgrimed eastern side of the grove. Here communion means fern, catbird, mosquito, poison ivy, moss, and pokeweed, forms that *melam* enters or becomes or sheds or embodies at will. For a tree—for the nymph whose life is the life of the tree—changeless truth is embodied in fluctuating forms. She makes epiphanies. I come to encounter them.

To make a vow to such a place is to stand with the ancients, who felt creation teeming with alert minds, tied votive ribbons on elder trees, and knew that oaths once heard underground would never be unsaid. They knew that nurse logs, fungi, and tree goddess roots grow right up out of death. Here on the path one year lay a baby raccoon, stayed from her last light steps, flowing in waves of beetles.

I am Phrasikleia: dying a maiden, I will be called maiden forever.
(Inscription of the Phrasikleia Kore)

From ancient tombstones to the laps of cedars, it is not paradox, but reality, that mercy streams from *memento mori* everywhere.

This morning, the rain-drenched mole carcass that has lain among the scaly leaves for days is sunken, deflated at last. It rained hard here all last night. When the hour comes, who will accompany these trees into the afterlife? They will enter the earth as an entourage together. And perhaps the mole has already gone ahead to make fertile their place.

The creatures sprinkled water on the corpse...Inanna rose.

Beside me, a weathered smooth placard, grey as sodden moleskin. Mute, it tilts on rusted leg, long erased of any written word. The tree it pointed toward is long gone.

But the sign evokes a tree the grove remembers, maiden forever, a tree as living and beloved to this circle as the ones who are still above ground. Her sister deities, above and below the earth, are listening still, for voices from vanishing libraries buried beside forgotten trails.

I wish this grove, this open-air shrine, to survive intact for the same reasons that we might dream that the people who knew what Cuyahoga means would wake beside a sparkling river, or the fragments of Sappho would resurrect fully whole. The word-root of *enigma* still means an opaque utterance and will always require intuitive wisdom to understand. It also signifies an opening. The grove provides no answer but an opening. The harpist is still touching her harp, poised to sound the next note.

If we sit within an arborvitae grove bowed low and listen:

The Spirit and the Nymphē say, Come.
(Revelations)

Endnotes

1. In a way. Since this is not an academic book, my translations are collages drawn loosely from various ancient sources, freely interpreted, abridged, expanded, or combined. Having wandered from their origins, they are creative rather than straightforward presentations. Word definitions are interpreted in context. Speaking of definitions: for clarity and simplicity in this book, myth is sacred story that conveys truth, and civilization is complex urban society. Song and poetry in early times were as one. Nymphs could be goddesses and goddesses could be nymphs, and I follow those fluid traditions.

2. Complete (and more literal) translations of ancient texts are listed in the Bibliography. Collections are easy to access in *The Electronic Text Corpus of Sumerian Literature* (ETCSL), and the *Perseus Digital Library* (for Greek and Latin). Greek and Latin translations are my own, while my presentations of Sumerian sources are improvisations upon texts in ETCSL, relying on the editors and translators J. Black, G. Cunningham, E. Fluckiger-Hawker, E. Robson, and G. Zólyomi. Akkadian details come from Benjamin Foster's *Before the Muses* and Stephanie Dalley's *Myths from Mesopotamia*. The source of Enki stories is Samuel Noah Kramer's *Myths of Enki, the Crafty God*. My portraits of Inanna owe much to the vision of Diane Wolkstein's *Inanna: Queen of Heaven and Earth* and Betty De Shong Meador's *Inanna, Lady of Largest Heart*. Artworks are identified by their titles in museums.

3. Kramer, *Myths of Enki*, 21.

4. Kramer, *Myths of Enki*, 116, 124-125.

5. Throughout this section I rely on the fragments edited and translated by Andrew George and Benjamin Foster in their editions of *The Epic of Gilgamesh*. I use the word hero only

in the ancient sense, as a semi-divine or mortal performer of extreme and memorable (not necessarily admirable) deeds, destined to suffer due to excessive divine love or hate, and worshipped in cult after death. In dying, heroes and heroines became immortal and were honored with ritual at sites important to their history. They remained powerful to punish or bless, and especially watched over human rites of transition.

6. This is how Andrew George renders the exclamation in *The Epic of Gilgamesh* (149); as he notes, other translations are possible.

7. Anna Goddeeris's article "Fields of Nippur" inspired and informed this discussion.

8. It is hard to speak about the silence of plant ethics. Michael Marder's *Plant-Thinking* and Stefano Mancuso's *The Revolutionary Genius of Plants* helped shape this provisional discussion.

Bibliography

Aeschylus I: The Persians, The Seven Against Thebes, The Suppliant Maidens, Prometheus Bound (3rd ed.), edited by David Grene and Richmond Lattimore. University of Chicago Press, 2013.

Aeschylus II: The Oresteia: Agamemnon, The Libation Bearers, The Eumenides (3rd ed.), edited by David Grene and Richmond Lattimore. University of Chicago Press, 2013.

Against the Grain: A Deep History of the Earliest States, James C. Scott. Yale University Press, 2017.

Akathist Hymn and Little Compline Arrangement: Greek and English Edition, Saint Romanos the Melodist. The Holy Convent of the Transfiguration of the Savior, 2015.

The Ancient Greek Hero in 24 Hours, Gregory Nagy. Belknap Press, 2013.

Ancient Perspectives: Maps and Their Place in Mesopotamia, Egypt, Greece, and Rome, edited by Richard J. A. Talbert. University of Chicago Press, 2012.

The Archaeology of Difference: Gender, Ethnicity, Class and the 'Other' in Antiquity, edited by Douglas R. Edwards and C. Thomas McCullough. American Schools of Oriental Research, 2007.

Aristotle: De Anima, translated by C. D. C. Reeve. Hackett, 2017.

Art of the First Cities: The Third Millennium B.C. from the Mediterranean to the Indus, Joan Aruz with Ronald Wallenfels. The Metropolitan Museum of Art, 2003.

The Art of Mesopotamia, Zainab Bahrani. Thames & Hudson, 2017.

Becoming Animal: An Earthly Cosmology, David Abram. Vintage Books, 2011.

Before the Muses: An Anthology of Akkadian Literature (3rd ed.), Benjamin R. Foster. CDL Press, 2005.

Belted Heroes and Bound Women: The Myth of the Homeric Warrior-King, Michael J. Bennett. Rowman & Littlefield, 1997.

Birth, Death, and Motherhood in Classical Greece, Nancy Demand. Johns Hopkins University Press, 1994.

Braiding Sweetgrass: Indigenous Wisdom, Scientific Knowledge, and the Teachings of Plants, Robin Wall Kimmerer. Milkweed Editions, 2013.

Bride of Hades to Bride of Christ: The Virgin and the Otherworldly Bridegroom in Ancient Greece and Early Christian Rome, Abbe Lind Walker. Routledge, 2020.

Catullus: The Poems, edited and translated by Peter Whigham. Penguin, 2006.

"The Cave at Vari I: Description, Account of Excavation, and History," Charles Heald Weller. *American Journal of Archaeology* Volume 7.3 (pp. 263-288). American Institute of Archaeology, 1903.

"The Cave at Vari II: Inscriptions," Maurice Edwards Dunham. *American Journal of Archaeology* Volume 7.3 (pp. 289-300). American Institute of Archaeology, 1903.

"The Cave at Vari III: Marble Reliefs," Ida Carleton Thallon. *American Journal of Archaeology* Volume 7.3 (pp. 301-319). American Institute of Archaeology, 1903.

Classical Mythology (11th ed.), Mark Morford, Robert J. Lenardon, and Michael Sham. Oxford University Press, 2018.

"Compensation," Ralph Waldo Emerson. In *The Spiritual Emerson: Essential Writings*, edited by David M. Robinson (pp. 110-130). Beacon Press, 2003.

Constraints of Desire: An Anthropology of Sex and Gender in Ancient Greece, John J. Winkler. Routledge, 1990.

"Cuyahoga River," *Encyclopedia of Cleveland History* [online]. Available at https://case.edu/ech/articles/c/cuyahoga-river Accessed 28 February 2022. Case Western Reserve University, 2022.

Dance and Ritual Play in Greek Religion, Steven H. Lonsdale. Johns Hopkins University Press, 1993.

"The Dance in Ancient Greece," Lillian Brady Lawler. *The*

Classical Journal Vol. 42.6 (pp. 343-349). The Classical Association of the Middle West and South, 1947.

"Dance in Textual Sources from Ancient Mesopotamia," Gabbay. *Near Eastern Archaeology* Vol. 66.3 (pp. 103-105). University of Chicago Press, 2003.

Dangerous Voices: Women's Laments and Greek Literature, Gail Holst-Warhaft. Routledge, 1992.

Descent to the Goddess: A Way of Initiation for Women, Sylvia Brinton Perera. Inner City Books, 1981.

"Devotionalism, Material Culture, and the Personal in Greek Religion," K. A. Rask. *Kernos* [online] Volume 29 (pp. 1-30). Available at http//journals.openedition.org/kernos/2386 Accessed 28 February 2022. Centre Internationale d'étude de la religion greque antique, 2016.

Did God Have a Wife? Archaeology and Folk Religion in Ancient Israel, William G. Dever. Eerdmans Publishing, 2005.

"Dressing the Neo-Assyrian Queen in Identity and Ideology: Elements and Ensembles from the Royal Tombs at Nimrud," Amy Rebecca Gansell. *American Journal of Archaeology* Volume 122.1 (pp. 65-100), American Institute of Archaeology, 2018.

The Electronic Text Corpus of Sumerian Literature [online], J. Black, G. Cunningham, E. Fluckiger-Hawker, E. Robson, and G. Zólyomi. Available at http://www-etcsl.orient.ox.ac.uk/ Accessed 24 February 2022. Oxford, 1998-.

Enuma Elish: The Babylonian Creation Epic (2nd ed.), Timothy J. Stephany. Published by Timothy J. Stephany, 2014.

Environmental Problems of the Greeks and Romans: Ecology in the Ancient Mediterranean, J. Donald Hughes. Johns Hopkins, 2014.

The Epic of Gilgamesh, translated by Danny P. Jackson. Bolchazy-Carducci, 2015.

The Epic of Gilgamesh: The Babylonian Epic Poem and Other Texts in Akkadian and Sumerian, edited by Andrew George. Penguin, 1999.

The Epic of Gilgamesh: A New Translation, Analogues, Criticism, Benjamin R. Foster. W.W. Norton & Company, 2001.

Eros at Dusk: Ancient Wedding and Love Poetry, Katherine Wasdin. Oxford University Press, 2018.

Euripides I: Alcestis, Medea, The Children of Heracles, Hippolytus (3rd ed.), edited by David Grene and Richmond Lattimore. University of Chicago Press, 2013.

Euripides III: Heracles, The Trojan Women, Iphigenia Among the Taurians, Ion (3rd ed.), edited by David Grene and Richmond Lattimore. University of Chicago Press, 2013.

Euripides IV: Helen, The Phoenician Women, Orestes (3rd ed.), edited by David Grene and Richmond Lattimore. University of Chicago Press, 2013.

Euripides V: Bacchae, Iphigenia in Aulis, The Cyclops, Rhesus (3rd ed.), edited by David Grene and Richmond Lattimore. University of Chicago Press, 2013.

The Evolution of the Gilgamesh Epic, Jeffrey H. Tigay. Bolchazy-Carducci, 2002.

"Fields of Nippur: Irrigation Districts and Lexicography in Old Babylonian Nippur," Anna Goddeeris. In *Topography and Toponymy in the Ancient Near East: Perspectives and Prospects* (pp. 97-112), edited by Jan Tavernier, Elynn Gorris, Kathleen Abraham, and Vanessa Boschloos. Peeters, 2018.

Finding the Mother Tree: Discovering the Wisdom of the Forest, Suzanne Simard. Knopf, 2021.

Flora Unveiled: The Discovery and Denial of Sex in Plants, Lincoln Taiz and Lee Taiz. Oxford University Press, 2017.

Gaia: A New Look at Life on Earth, James Lovelock. Oxford University Press, 1979.

"Gendered Sexuality in Sumerian Love Poetry," Jerrold S. Cooper, in *Sumerian Gods and Their Representation* (pp. 84-97), edited by Irving L. Fenkel and Markham. J. Geller. University of Antwerp Center for Dutch Language and Speech, 1997.

Gender and Immortality: Heroines in Ancient Greek Myth *and Cult,*

Deborah Lyons. Princeton University Press, 1997.

Gender and the Interpretation of Classical Myth, Lillian E. Doherty. Duckworth, 2001.

Gilgamesh and the Huluppu-Tree: A Reconstructed Sumerian Text, Samuel N. Kramer. The Oriental Institute and University of Chicago Press, 1938.

The Goddess with Uplifted Arms in Cyprus, Vassos Karageorghis. Gleerup, 1977.

"The Greek Cult of the Nymphs at Corinth," Theodora Kopestonsky. *Hesperia: The Journal of the American School of Classical Studies at Athens* Volume 85.4 (pp. 711-777). The American School of Classical Studies at Athens, 2016.

Greek Nymphs: Myth, Cult, Lore, Jennifer Larson. Oxford University Press, 2001.

The Greek Plant World in Myth, Art and Literature, Hellmut Baumann, translated by William Stearn and Eldwyth Ruth Stearn. Timber Press, 1993.

Greek Religion, Walter Burkert. Blackwell, 1985.

The Harps that Once...: Sumerian Poetry in Translation, Thorkild Jacobsen. Yale University Press, 1997.

The Heartbeat of Trees: Embracing Our Ancient Bond with Forests and Nature, Peter Wohlleben. Greystone Books, 2021.

Heaven on Earth: Temples, Ritual, and Cosmic Symbolism in the Ancient World, Deena Ragavan. Oriental Institute of the University of Chicago, 2013.

The Hebrew Goddess (3rd ed.), Raphael Patai. Wayne State University Press, 1990.

Helen of Troy: The Story Behind the Most Beautiful Woman in the World, Bettany Hughes. Random House, 2005.

The Hero with a Thousand Faces (3rd ed.), Joseph Campbell. New World Library, 2008.

Hesiod: Theogony, Works and Days, Shield (2nd ed.), translated by Apostolos N. Athanassakis. Johns Hopkins University Press, 2004.

The Hidden Life of Trees: What They Feel, How They Communicate: Discoveries from a Secret World, Peter Wohlleben. Greystone Books, 2016.

Hippocratic Writings, edited by G. E. R. Lloyd. Penguin, 1978.

The Homeric Hymn to Demeter: Translation, Commentary, and Interpretive Essays, edited by Helene P. Foley. Princeton University Press, 1994.

The Homeric Hymns (2nd ed.), translated by Apostolos N. Athanassakis. Johns Hopkins University Press, 2004.

Horace: Satires and Epistles, edited by John Davie and Robert Cowan. Oxford University Press, 2011.

I Am Ashurbanipal, King of the World, King of Assyria, edited by Gareth Brereton. Thames & Hudson with the British Museum, 2018.

Idle Weeds: The Life of an Ohio Sandstone Ridge, David Rains Wallace. Ohio State University Press, 1980.

If Not, Winter: Fragments of Sappho, translated by Anne Carson. Vintage Books, 2003.

The Iliad of Homer, translated by Richmond Lattimore. University of Chicago Press, 2011.

The Imagination of Plants: A Book of Botanical Mythology, Matthew Hall. State University Of New York, 2019.

"Inanna and the Huluppu Tree: One Way of Demoting a Great Goddess," Johanna Stuckey. In *Feminist Poetics of the Sacred: Creative Suspicions*, edited by Frances Devlin-Glass and Lyn McCredden (pp. 91-105). Oxford University Press, 2000.

Inanna, Lady of Largest Heart: Poems of the Sumerian High Priestess Enheduanna, Betty De Shong Meador. University of Texas Press, 2000.

Inanna, Queen of Heaven and Earth: Her Stories and Hymns from Sumer, Diane Wolkstein and Samuel Noah Kramer. Harper Perennial, 1983.

In the Wake of the Goddesses: Women, Culture and the Biblical Transformation of Pagan Myth, Tikva Frymer-Kensky. Fawcett

Columbine, 1992.

An Introduction to Akkadian Literature: Contexts and Content, Alan Lenzi. Eisenbrauns, 2019.

An Introduction to Ancient Mesopotamian Religion, Tammi J. Schneider. Eerdmans, 2011.

"Julian and the Last Oracle at Delphi." Timothy Gregory. *Greek, Roman and Byzantine Studies* Volume 24.4 (pp. 355-366), Duke University Libraries, 1983.

"Landscapes of Artemis," Susan Guettel Cole. *The Classical World* 93.5 (pp. 471-481). Johns Hopkins University Press on behalf of The Classical Association of the Atlantic States, 2000.

Landscapes, Gender, and Ritual Space: The Ancient Greek Experience, Susan Guettel Cole. University of California Press, 2004.

"The Life and Health of Assyrian Queens," Tracy Spurrier. *The Ancient Near East Today: Current News About the Ancient Past*, Volume 3.6. Available at https://www.asor.org/anetoday/2015/06/the-life-and-health-of-assyrian-queens/ Accessed 28 February 2022. Friends of the American Society of Overseas Research, 2015.

The Literature of Ancient Sumer, translated by Jeremy Black, Graham Cunningham, Eleanor Robson, and Gábor Zólyomi. Oxford University Press, 2005.

Longus: Daphis and Chloe, translated by Paul Turner. Penguin, 1989.

The Looting of the Iraq Museum, Baghdad: The Lost Legacy of Ancient Mesopotamia, edited by Angela M. H. Schuster and Milbry Polk. Harry N. Abrams, 2005.

Lucretius: The Nature of Things, translated by A. E. Stallings. Penguin, 2007.

"The Marginalization of the Goddesses," Tikva Frymer-Kensky. In *Gilgamesh: A Reader* (pp. 95-108), edited by John Maier. Bolchazy-Carducci, 1997.

Marriage to Death: The Conflation of Wedding and Funeral Rituals in

Greek Tragedy, Rush Rehm. Princeton University Press, 2019.

Melusine of Lusignan and the Cult of the Faery Woman, Gareth Knight. Skylight Press, 2013.

Mesopotamia: The Invention of the City, Gwendoyn Leick. Penguin, 2001.

Mythago Wood, Robert Holdstock. Orb Books, 2003.

The Mythology of Plants: Botanical Lore from Ancient Greece and Rome, Annette Giesecke. J. Paul Getty Museum, 2014.

Myths from Mesopotamia: Creation, the Flood, Gilgamesh, and Others (revised ed.), Stephanie Dalley. Oxford University Press, 2000.

Myths of Enki, the Crafty God, Samuel Noah Kramer. Oxford University Press, 1989.

Mycelium Running: How Mushrooms Can Help Save the World, Paul Stamets. Ten Speed Press, 2005.

The Myth of the Eternal Return: Cosmos and History (reprint ed.), Mircea Eliade, translated by Willard Trask. Princeton University Press, 2018.

The Odyssey of Homer, translated by Richmond Lattimore. Harper Perennial, 2007.

Other Minds: The Octopus, the Sea, and the Deep Origins of Consciousness, Peter Godfrey-Smith. Farrar, Straus and Giroux, 2016.

Ovid: Metamorphoses, translated by Rolfe Humphries. Indiana University Press, 2018.

The Oxford Classical Dictionary (3rd ed.), edited by Simon Hornblower and Antony Spawforth. Oxford University Press, 1996.

Pausanias: Description of Greece: Arcadia, Boeotia, Phocis, and Ozolian Locri, translated by W. H. S. Jones. Harvard University Press, 1935.

Perseus Digital Library [online], Gregory Crane and Tufts University. Available at https://www.loc.gov/item/lcwaN0003879/ Accessed 24 February 2022. Tufts University, 2001-.

Plato: Phaedrus, translated by Alexander Nehamas and Paul Woodruff. Hackett, 1995.

Plato: Timaeus and Critias, translated by Robin Waterfield. Oxford University Press, 2008.

Plants as Persons: A Philosophical Botany, Matthew Hall. SUNY Press, 2011.

Plant-Thinking: A Philosophy of Vegetal Life, Michael Marder. Columbia University Press, 2013.

The Power of Thetis: Allusion and Interpretation in the Iliad, Laura M. Slatkin. University of California Press, 1991.

The Pregnant Virgin: A Process of Psychological Transformation, Marion Woodman. Inner City Books, 1985.

The Presocratics, edited by Philip Wheelwright. Prentice Hall, 1997.

Princess, Priestess, Poet: The Sumerian Temple Hymns of Enheduanna, Betty De Shong Meador. University of Texas Press, 2009.

Reinventing Eden: The Fate of Nature in Western Culture, Carolyn Merchant. Routledge, 2004.

The Revolutionary Genius of Plants: A New Understanding of Plant Intelligence and Behavior, Stefano Mancuso. Atria Books, 2017.

A Serpentine Path: Mysteries of the Goddess, Carol P. Christ. Far Press, 2016.

Sex and Eroticism in Mesopotamian Literature, Gwendolyn Leick. Routledge, 1994.

The Singer of Tales (2nd ed.), Albert B. Lord. Harvard University Press, 2000.

Sophocles I: Oedipus the King, Oedipus at Colonus, Antigone (3rd ed.), edited by David Grene, Richmond Lattimore, Mark Griffith, and Glenn Most. University of Chicago Press, 2013.

Sophocles II: Ajax, The Women of Trachis, Electra, Philoctetes, The Trackers (3rd ed.), edited by David Grene, Richmond Lattimore, Mark Griffith, and Glenn Most. University of Chicago Press, 2013.

The Spell of the Sensuous: Perception and Language in a More-Than-

Human World, David Abram. Vintage Books, 1996.

Sumerian Mythology: A Study of Spiritual and Literary Achievement in the Third Millennium B.C. (revised ed.), Samuel Noah Kramer. University of Pennsylvania Press, 1972.

The Transformation of Hera, Joan V. O'Brien. Rowman & Littlefield, 1993.

The Treasures of Darkness: A History of Mesopotamian Religion, Thorkild Jacobsen. Yale University Press, 1976.

Treasures from the Royal Tombs of Ur, edited by Richard L. Zettler and Lee Horne. University of Pennsylvania Museum, 1998.

Trees: A Complete Guide to Their Biology and Structure, Roland Ennos. Comstock Publishing, 2016.

Virgil: The Aeneid, translated by W. F. Jackson Knight. Penguin, 1958.

Walden, Henry David Thoreau. Shambhala Publications, 2008.

"Water System," Willis Sibley. *Encyclopedia of Cleveland History* [online]. Available at https://case.edu/ech/articles/w/water-system Accessed 28 February 2022. Case Western Reserve University, 2022.

"Why Did Enki Organize the World," H. L. J. Vanstiphout. In *Sumerian Gods and Their Representation* (pp. 117-133), edited by Irving L. Fenkel and Markham J. Geller. University of Antwerp Center for Dutch Language and Speech, 1997.

Wild Apples (reprint ed.), Henry David Thoreau. American Roots, 2015.

Wildwood: A Journey through Trees, Roger Deakin. Free Press, 2007.

The Wisdom of the Desert: Sayings from the Desert Fathers of the Fourth Century, Thomas Merton. New Directions, 1960.

Woman and Nature: The Roaring Inside Her, Susan Griffin. Counterpoint, 1978.

The Woman and the Lyre: Women Writers in Classical Greece and Rome, Jane McIntosh Snyder. Southern Illinois University Press, 1989.

"A Woman's History of Warfare," Ellen O'Gorman. In *Laughing with Medusa* (pp. 189-208), edited by Vanda Zajko and Miriam Leonard. Oxford University Press, 2008.

Women in Mycenaean Greece: The Linear B Tablets from Pylos and Knossos, Barbara Olsen. Routledge, 2014.

Women in the Ancient World, Jenifer Neils. Getty Publications, 2011.

Women of Babylon: Gender and Representation in Mesopotamia, Zainab Bahrani. Routledge, 2001.

Women's Work, the First 20,000 Years: Women, Cloth, and Society in Early Times, Elizabeth Wayland Barber. W. W. Norton & Company, 1994.

"The Worst Mistake in the History of the Human Race," Jared Diamond. In *Classic Readings in Cultural Anthropology* (4th ed.), edited by Gary Ferraro (pp. 37-42). Cengage Learning, 2015.

Your Inner Fish: A Journey Into the 3.5-Billion-Year History of the Human Body, Neil Shubin. Vintage Books, 2009.

Author Biography

Dianna Rhyan is a mythologist and therapist whose work focuses on forgotten voices, nature goddesses, and the spirituality of sacred landscapes. At the age of eight she created her first secret language on tablets of clay made from the creek beside her home. In time that language grew into a PhD in Ancient Greek and Latin, and thirty years of college teaching. She has been a visiting scholar on archaeological excavations in Greece and Cyprus, where she explored women's devotion to rural shrines, and investigated the ancient evidence for women's veils. When not delving into archaic myth or studying Sumerian, she can be found exploring the Cuyahoga Valley trails of Northeast Ohio with her swift-footed husband, her hiking crone companions, and assorted wise dogs.

Acknowledgments

I would like to thank the forested park with its singing creek that filled my childhood days, and the fifth-grade teacher who handed me my first real book of ancient mythology. Christine who stayed and then trusted me with her rare copy of *Life on a Sandstone Ridge*. The clock tower on the island of Poros, the chapel of Agios Dimitrios on the brow of Akrokorinth, and the fountain of Hadji Mustafa on the way. Saul who understood quest, Max the adventurer, and parents who filled a home with books and music. In different seasons, Dawes Arboretum, the Hocking Hills, Stan Hywet Hall & Gardens, and the trails of the Cuyahoga Valley National Park. Ron, Julie, and Brian for gracious welcomes to enchanting interdisciplinary studies, archives, and gardens. My responsive and expert team at Moon Books, especially my supportive and perceptive editors Frank Smecker and Trevor Greenfield. They believed in this project and made it possible for years of journals about the Cuyahoga Valley to become this book. Receptive readers Nicholas, Mark, Lisa, Emily, Chris, Ahna, and Tamar; forest guardians Shelley and John. The intrepid nature spirits Gloria and Dawna hold my heartfelt gratitude, for they heard every word of this journey unfold on trails as we joyfully wore out hiking boots together. Nicholas of Byzantium, leaping in Nafplio, reimagining ruined fortresses into profound new being, and crossing the stone bridge near hemlock ravine. Mark the Mystic Ultra, whose compassion, wisdom, and loving patience run so deep as to be worthy of myth. There you stand, looking east to the trail, in the sunlight near Pine Hollow on the Sound of Music hill.

MOON
BOOKS

PAGANISM & SHAMANISM

What is Paganism? A religion, a spirituality, an alternative belief system, nature worship? You can find support for all these definitions (and many more) in dictionaries, encyclopaedias, and text books of religion, but subscribe to any one and the truth will evade you. Above all Paganism is a creative pursuit, an encounter with reality, an exploration of meaning and an expression of the soul. Druids, Heathens, Wiccans and others, all contribute their insights and literary riches to the Pagan tradition. Moon Books invites you to begin or to deepen your own encounter, right here, right now.

If you have enjoyed this book, why not tell other readers by posting a review on your preferred book site.

Recent bestsellers from Moon Books are:

Journey to the Dark Goddess
How to Return to Your Soul
Jane Meredith
Discover the powerful secrets of the Dark Goddess and
transform your depression, grief and pain into healing
and integration.
Paperback: 978-1-84694-677-6 ebook: 978-1-78099-223-5

Shamanic Reiki
Expanded Ways of Working with Universal Life Force Energy
Llyn Roberts, Robert Levy
Shamanism and Reiki are each powerful ways of healing; together,
their power multiplies. *Shamanic Reiki* introduces techniques to
help healers and Reiki practitioners tap ancient healing wisdom.
Paperback: 978-1-84694-037-8 ebook: 978-1-84694-650-9

Pagan Portals – The Awen Alone
Walking the Path of the Solitary Druid
Joanna van der Hoeven
An introductory guide for the solitary Druid, *The Awen Alone* will
accompany you as you explore, and seek out your own place
within the natural world.
Paperback: 978-1-78279-547-6 ebook: 978-1-78279-546-9

A Kitchen Witch's World of Magical Herbs & Plants
Rachel Patterson
A journey into the magical world of herbs and plants, filled with
magical uses, folklore, history and practical magic. By popular
writer, blogger and kitchen witch, Tansy Firedragon.
Paperback: 978-1-78279-621-3 ebook: 978-1-78279-620-6

Medicine for the Soul
The Complete Book of Shamanic Healing
Ross Heaven
All you will ever need to know about shamanic healing and how to
become your own shaman...
Paperback: 978-1-78099-419-2 ebook: 978-1-78099-420-8

Shaman Pathways – The Druid Shaman
Exploring the Celtic Otherworld
Danu Forest
A practical guide to Celtic shamanism with exercises and
techniques as well as traditional lore for exploring the Celtic
Otherworld.
Paperback: 978-1-78099-615-8 ebook: 978-1-78099-616-5

Traditional Witchcraft for the Woods and Forests
A Witch's Guide to the Woodland with Guided Meditations and
Pathworking
Mélusine Draco
A Witch's guide to walking alone in the woods, with guided
meditations and pathworking.
Paperback: 978-1-84694-803-9 ebook: 978-1-84694-804-6

Wild Earth, Wild Soul
A Manual for an Ecstatic Culture
Bill Pfeiffer
Imagine a nature-based culture so alive and so connected,
spreading like wildfire. This book is the first flame...
Paperback: 978-1-78099-187-0 ebook: 978-1-78099-188-7

Naming the Goddess
Trevor Greenfield
Naming the Goddess is written by over eighty adherents and
scholars of Goddess and Goddess Spirituality.
Paperback: 978-1-78279-476-9 ebook: 978-1-78279-475-2

Shapeshifting into Higher Consciousness
Heal and Transform Yourself and Our World with Ancient
Shamanic and Modern Methods
Llyn Roberts
Ancient and modern methods that you can use every day to
transform yourself and make a positive difference in the world.
Paperback: 978-1-84694-843-5 ebook: 978-1-84694-844-2

Readers of ebooks can buy or view any of these bestsellers by
clicking on the live link in the title. Most titles are published in
paperback and as an ebook. Paperbacks are available in traditional
bookshops. Both print and ebook formats are available online.

Find more titles and sign up to our readers' newsletter at
http://www.johnhuntpublishing.com/paganism
Follow us on Facebook at https://www.facebook.com/MoonBooks
and Twitter at https://twitter.com/MoonBooksJHP